Accelerated Learning Techniques for a Budding Sociopath

Accelerated Learning Techniques for a Budding Sociopath

A Bunch of Short Stories

EVAN HUNDHAUSEN

Tome Publishing, LTD.

&

Lotza Marketing, LLC.

Accelerated Learning Techniques for a Budding Sociopath
A Bunch of Short Stories

Tome Publishing, LTD.
Lotza Marketing, LLC.

Front and back book cover design, book layout and production by
Evan Hundhausen   and   D D Stewart.

No Fuglies for Fritz Kramer was first published in another form in *The
Project for a New Mythology: Volume 1, Issue 4.*

Sham Pain, a short screenplay, was a semi-finalist in *The Moondance
International Film Festival* in 2004.

Yes, I wear a Man Purse, cover image, bb0011 – Man Purse, provided
courtesy of D D Stewart, ©2016 David Stewart

Manufactured through CreateSpace.com

First Edition: January 10, 2018

ISBN-13:978-0-9986287-4-5
Please REVIEW this Book on Amazon!

ACKNOWLEDGEMENTS

First, I would like to thank all my friends at my writers' groups; the Boulder Novel Writer's Workshop and the Writers Idea Factory for all their critique and support. Thanks to Jeffry Weiss for showing me how to self-publish on Amazon, thanks to David Stewart for encouraging me to "take over the world" and thanks to my family for encouraging me to be an artist, writer, musician and whatever else I had a passion for during all my childhood through today.

REVIEW PAGE

"I'm very happy they let Evan out of the home on occasion in order to wander among normal people and ply his trade, which is writing. Evan travels to the beat of a different drum. He lives in the realm of the bizarre, the world between regular people doing regular things, and science fiction. I would swear he studied under Rod Serling ("The Twilight Zone") but Rod never had Evan's sense of humor. His stories will make you laugh or cause some sleepless nights . . . but they will surely touch your heart and mind. I eagerly await Evan's next story. I just hope they let him out of the home long enough to write a full-length novel." Jeffry Weiss - Author of the Paul Decker series of political thrillers which can be found on Amazon.

"I've read several of Evan's work, and the reason I like it is the noir-type quirkiness, science fiction feel. It always gives me this classic sense of old school Fitzgerald, Hemingway, while still being contemporary speculative. Comical in its eccentricity but very original and modern while maintaining a classic feel. That's what great writing does. That's what Evan can give you. Tales that last." - Brandon Berntson, Horror Writer and Author of the Snap Dragon Series.

"For as long as I have known Evan (about a quarter of a century), he has been a true artist in multiple fields, but especially, IMO, in his writing. Evan always had the proper combination of a unique, original look on the world, devotion to constantly improving himself at his craft, and drive to be successful in his creative endeavors, that make a great artist, no matter what the medium. - Mike-o Martelli, Poet

Dear Reader,

In all honesty, the title of this book came about from a friend who blurted it out one day when we were joking about book titles and I used it purely because it grabbed attention.

The characters here are all sociopaths in their own way; manipulating, self-serving, thinking they must survive above all else in their worlds because when all you know is that, *that's just the way it is!* How could you possibly have the patience or gumption to go look and learn to see if there is even another way?

Google defines *so·ci·o·path* as "a person with a personality disorder manifesting itself in extreme antisocial attitudes and behavior and a lack of conscience."

Personally, my definition of the word sociopath is different. I'm more interested in the "corporate" sociopath. Example; the person in power who's decided that listening to their conscience will not do them any good when it comes down to the bottom line or the paycheck they get on Friday.

Maybe sociopaths grow up without going to church on Sunday. Maybe sociopaths commit small crimes as a youngster and get away with it so often it makes them the person they are today.

From manipulating Wall Street, to running countries, to making Christmas dinner for the whole family... sociopaths are everywhere!

Do you get along very well in "society" without a hitch? Do people think you're a good person and nice to others?   Congratulations!   You most likely are your own special kind of sociopath.

If you don't think about who you are, in relation to being a good person at all, then you just might be a sociopath. If you don't think about it at all then you probably are one.

If you think you can take all the toys up to Heaven with you when you die, you should remember this, when you step inside an Egyptian pyramid you'll find the Pharaoh's treasures were stolen and pilfered a long time ago and all that's left is a dead body and the writings on the wall.

It's probably normal to ruminate over whether the title of your book works, but recently I was stoned, and I realized it works just fine. It was just a feeling I got, and it put a smile on my face.

My hope is you will like these stories, that they will entertain you, because to hope for anything more in a book you write is something only a sociopath would do.

Sincerely,

Evan Hundhausen

Author

Join the newsletter : http://eepurl.com/buVFCT

TABLE OF CONTENTS

Elnora and the Man
A SHORT STORY

EVAN
HUNDHAUSEN

ELNORA AND THE MAN

"Do you know how hard it is to find fruit without the letter p in it at a grocery store?" Elnora asked the man sitting next to her at the bar.

The man stared as Elnora downed the rest of her drink. She looked back at him briefly, then raised her hand to order another one.

"You have plums, peaches, pears, apples, pomegranates, and not to mention how careful I have to be when I order a drink!" Elnora said. "One time, this guy ordered me a fuzzy navel and I had to turn it down."

"I'm allergic myself," the man finally said thinking it wouldn't divulge very much. "I take vitamin supplements instead," he added.

Elnora was becoming a sloppy drunk. She laughed before turning back to the drink the bartender placed in front of her.

"Every day, I begin a new hobby in hopes of meeting someone," Elnora rambled on. "Jogging in Central Park one day, yoga the next, personal ads, I even go to different churches on Sundays.

"Once, I found myself at a dance class at an old person's home. All the elderly women stared as men with canes asked me to dance. 'I can't eat fruit with p's in them!' I told one elderly man.

"He invited me back to his room. 'I have a kiwi you can have. It was given to me by my grandson earlier today!' he assured me.

"When the old man bent down to open his small refrigerator, I noticed a bottle of prune juice. The refrigerator light made it seem like it was wearing a halo. I fell to the floor sobbing at the sight. The old man's hand was unable to console me."

The man next to her ran his hand over the smooth surface of the bar wondering how to continue conversing with this attractive woman. He noticed her bosom. She wore a yellow outfit and the man couldn't help but be reminded of the pineapple sherbet he'd seen the other day at an organic supermarket. He didn't buy it and eat it like he wanted to.

"So why can't you eat any fruit with p's in them?" the man managed to say despite his growing uneasiness.

The woman turned, swiveling her barstool in his direction. She leaned into his face and laughed. The man smelled the whiskey on her breath. Normally, the behavior would have offended him, but this woman was allergic to fruit like he was.

"You won't believe me," she finally said.

"I'll believe anything," the man replied.

"I get a reaction to it."

"A reaction?" he asked.

"I should've never brought it up." She threw her head down into her arms dramatically.

As fast as she had dropped it, Elnora lifted her head and continued. "One night, I revealed my secret to three young men at a club. 'Prove it,' they said. 'We want to see it!' They bought different fruit liquors, peach schnapps, and ciders. Hovering over me, they poured each drink down my throat, splashing them on my face and clothes. Humiliated, I ran out of the club. I stopped at one point on the street to put my finger into my mouth to puke.

"I felt alone once again. I cried and floated home on a

stream of my own tears."

"It's okay. You don't have to talk about it, miss," the man told her. He was moved, yet shocked by what she had said. "I don't meet too many people like myself who are allergic to fruit is all.

"Although I've been to many support groups where people are allergic to all sorts of things," the man continued.

"One man's eyes would puff up like he'd been in a boxing match if he ate chocolate and one woman would get red rashes all over her body if she had shellfish," he recollected. "Except for one person allergic to bananas, I've never met anyone with a problem like mine, so I've kept it to myself for a long time, but tonight, with you sitting here beside me..." the man stopped. He was embarrassed by what he'd just said.

Elnora's head bobbed up from the bar like a marionette. The fuzzy feeling of whiskey fabricated an answer, a solution, for her on this night.

"You have to come home with me," she told the man.

He was barely able to pull out money and pay for the drinks as Elnora tugged him in the direction of the door.

Outside, they walked down the street arm in arm. Elnora pressed into him. Goosebumps covered the man's skin, excited by the woman's touch.

They passed a grocery store. A fruit and produce stand lined the front. Picking up an apple, a plum, and a pear, Elnora handed them to the man.

"I thought you were allergic to these?" he exclaimed. Elnora just laughed and went into the store to pay.

They continued walking down the sidewalk with the plastic bag full of ripe fruit tapping against the man's leg.

Holding the bag annoyed him and he handed it back to Elnora.

"So," Elnora began, taking the bag. "What kind of reaction do you get?"

"I'd prefer not to talk about it," the man admitted, feeling uncomfortable about her buying all the fruit.

Across the street, a Broadway play let out and the theater's patrons exited the building slowly, like a toothpaste tube oozing out its paste. Roaring reviews lit up the marquee about its current production. *Four stars!* and *A must see!!* blinked above the exiting crowd.

Soon the couple's walk ended and Elnora arrived at her two-story brownstone. The man followed her up the steps and into her apartment. He watched her bolt the door behind them. Then, he followed her to the kitchen and watched Elnora wash the fruit under the sink's faucet.

Elnora brought an apple up to her lips and without warning, bit into it. Before the man could ask why she'd done it, she started to float in the air. She rose to the ceiling and bumped her head. She rubbed it with her hand and laughed.

The man turned and exited the kitchen without saying a word. Elnora followed him out, floating as she was.

"Where are you going?" she asked, but got no answer.

He climbed the stairs to the second floor and walked into the first room he encountered. A bedroom. There was a birdcage in the corner and inside, two canaries flapped their wings in surprise at the man entering. Posters of airplanes, birds, skydivers, snowboarders, and even superheroes decorated the walls.

"What are you doing?" he heard Elnora ask behind him. He turned towards her and looked at her floating in the space that was the bedroom doorway.

"I'm just checking your place out," he answered.

Elnora floated over to the birdcage and opened the door. It creaked open and the birds flew out.

***

The two canaries perched on the chandelier above the dining room table. The table was set with plates, silverware, and cloth napkins with holders.

Elnora had since stopped floating in the air. She now sat across from him at the table pouring the man a cup of tea from a teapot.

"So, you never told me," Elnora said. "What *kind* of allergic reaction do you get?"

The man did not respond immediately. He sipped his tea for a moment.

"Once, in elementary school during lunchtime, I found a purple plum my mom had packed for me in my lunchbox. I ate it and suddenly found myself sitting up in the rafters of the cafeteria. The maintenance man finally came along with a ladder to get me down. From then on, I despised fruit. Every time my mom packed it in my lunchbox, I threw it out.

"There was another time when I was visiting my grandmother. I sat under her apple tree in the backyard reading a book. A ripe red apple fell on my head like I was Isaac Newton. I lost interest in the book and began to throw apples back into the tree. More fell to the ground as I hit the branches with the fallen apples. I played this game thinking I would bring in an armful and grandmother would bake pies.

"Finally, I picked up an apple and wiped it against my jeans. I brought it to my mouth and bit into it. My grandmother later found me up high in the apple tree. I was so high she had to call the fire department to get me down."

The man finished his story and suddenly began to rise out of his chair. He grabbed the tablecloth and the silverware, plates, teapot, and cups crashed to the floor while he rose to the ceiling. The chandelier shook as he hit it with his head and the birds flapped their wings and flew around him.

"That was passion fruit tea you drank," Elnora said matter-of-factly, but playfully, as if she had known his secret all along.

Elnora rose out of her chair and floated next to him with her back hitting the ceiling.

"It smelled fruity to me, but I drank it anyway because of you," the embarrassed man said, watching the excited canaries fly around them. The birds stopped in mid-flight, twisting their heads to the side and curiously chirping at the man.

Elnora held out an apple. Her bite marks on it had turned yellowish and brown. He took it from her hand and bit into it, not seeming to mind at all.

A STEAMPUNK SHORT STORY

DESTINY ALEXIS &
THE ROBOT 3000

EVAN HUNDHAUSEN

~ *Dedication* ~

I'd like to dedicate this short story to the memory to my deceased cousin, Jennifer. When we were children she announced at the dinner table at our grandparent's house, "When I have a baby, I'm going to name her Destiny Alexis!" Everyone marveled how she could come up with such an imaginative name. I never forgot it.

Later in life, my cousin had two wonderful children of her own: Nathan and Rosa. She did not name her daughter Destiny Alexis, but instead, named her in memory of her aunt and my mother, Rosa.

DESTINY ALEXIS AND THE ROBOT 3000

Destiny Alexis took out her inhaler, pressed it, and breathed in. She was thinking about a dark subject because her grandfather was now on his *deathbed*, or at least that was what her mother told her.

Where do you find a "death bed?" the girl thought to herself. *There must be a store that sells 'em!*

She held a dandelion in her hand. It felt wet, soft, even mushy as she pulled the tiny petals apart with her fingers in a bunch.

"What do you know about death?" she asked the R3K that stood above her as she sat on the tree stump in her grandfather's garden.

"Death," the R3K began. "The end of life; the total and permanent cessation of all the vital functions of an organism"

"No," the nine-year-old girl interrupted the robot.

"What do you personally know about death?"

"I have no spirit like you do, Destiny Alexis," the R3K replied.

"Duh," she bent her brow in annoyance, then stood up and threw the destroyed dandelion to the ground.

"Let's go find some squirrels!" she announced. "We'll walk down the trail and find some, okay? They're in the trees. They're taking their acorns into the trees. That's where they store them. They fill their cute little faces with acorns and then store them in holes in the trees!"

The R3K's metal eyes blinked with red light and it followed the girl as she skipped down the path wandering deeper into her grandfather's garden, which sat at the edge of a forest that etched down the mountain. The metal legs of the Robot 3000 creaked as it went along after her.

"That whirring sound you can hear a mile away, Mr. Tin Man!"

Ever since Destiny Alexis' Grandpa showed her the old movie *The Wizard of OZ*, she called the R3K Tin Man.

"You'd be horrible to have around for a hunting party!" Destiny said. "All the foxes would hear you coming from a mile away and the hunting party would never catch one fox. All the hunters up on their horses would be real mad at you!"

***

The girl's mother was inside the house and her father known as Harry laid in bed, while Destiny Alexis' mother sat beside him.

"Have you told us about all the bank accounts, Father?" she asked.

"Hmmmmmm . . . did you say something, Margaret?" Harry lay there with the covers up to his neck.

"The accounts, Father," Margaret repeated. "Are there any more you haven't told us about?"

Harry's brow bent in disapproval.

"Ridiculous!" he said. "Of course I've told you about all of them! Ridiculous!"

But Grandpa Harry hadn't told her about everything though. In fact, he'd decided to keep several things secret.

The R3K had helped him write the most important element of his will. It was the treasure map for his granddaughter Destiny Alexis. The R3K had buried the box in the front yard for her to dig up after his death, which Harry wished would be soon.

Better for a robot to keep your secrets than any human! Harry thought to himself in the bed. *How wonderful a time my granddaughter will have reading the treasure map and digging up the box and discovering what is inside!*

***

Out front, in the woods, hidden by shrubs and trees, Destiny Alexis skipped along the path.

"I want to go off alone!" she cried watching the R3K slowly trailing behind with legs creaking. "Do you understand? You hunk of junk, you?"

"My job is to watch you, Destiny Alexis," the R3K said.

"No, it's not!" the girl yelled back. "You're supposed to be taking care of Grandpa Harry. Not me!"

"You are correct, Destiny Alexis." The soft neon red bulbs inside the two large eyes of the robot's head lit up as it replied to the girl.

"I have been given a command prompt to be your babysitter, Destiny Alexis," the R3K continued. "This is what I must do."

"Well then," the girl smiled mischievously, "let's see if

you can keep up with me, you old clunker! Clunk, clunk, clunk!"

The robot moved one mechanical leg in front of the other to keep up.

Sounds of running water could be heard coming from further down the path and Destiny Alexis ran faster towards the sound, excited. Destiny finally ended up at the bands of a stream. She took her shoes off and waded into the water.

"Be careful, Destiny Alexis," the R3K said.

"What do you know about it?" the girl snapped back. "You can't go in the stream can you? You don't want to electrocute yourself!"

"My parts are waterproof, but I have been programmed to only go into water in emergencies and that is all."

"You mean if I'm drowning?"

"Yes, Destiny Alexis. Correct."

The girl heard a rustle of tree branches coming from down the path the way they had come. It was her mother. She wore a long red dress and a large red hat with a black feather in it. She walked towards the child and the robot in her black boots.

"Destiny Alexis!" Her mother held onto the skirt of her dress with both hands as she came to edge of the stream. "What are you doing?"

"I'm wading, Mother."

"Well, get out. You don't want to get your dress wet."

Destiny Alexis didn't like being told what to do. Her mother made her put the dress on this morning. They both arrived by train in the small town of Motorson, named after her Grandfather, the great robot inventor, Harry Motorson.

The girl had slept on the train all night long and in the morning, she ate a breakfast of oatmeal with milk, jelly, and butter.

She chose marmalade from a selection of jelly packets in a white saucer on her table. The jelly packets were in tiny plastic tubs and she picked the marmalade over strawberry and grape. She thought the flavor was a little bitter compared to the fruit jellies, but she liked it anyway.

Now the girl and her mother were both at Grandpa's house and so far wading in the stream was the most fun she'd had since her arrival. Selecting marmalade from the jelly packets that morning being the only other exception maybe.

"Mother just wants to spoil it all," the girl said to the R3K as she walked out of the stream and back up to her shoes sitting on the bank.

***

Back at the house, Harry talked to the executor of his estate who sat in one of the chairs alongside his bed.

The man sitting there held a pipe in his hand, unlit. Harry, despite being bedridden, was still the acting director of the Motorson Company.

"Chase!" Harry said. "When are you going to combine the Robot 3000 and the Robotica Love Model into one robot?"

"Combine the R3K with the Love Bot?" Chase asked, motioning in an animated fashion towards Harry with the hand holding the pipe.

Grandpa Harry responded, "I fondly recall how the Robotica Female Love Model sung me to sleep at night and massaged my back when I wanted it to. What I liked most was how the Love Model said my name. It always sounded just like a lover should. At least I got that detail right."

Chase thought about what Grandpa Harry said. He himself had never owned a Love Model, but he knew every single detail about the machine because he oversaw all the production of it at the factory.

"The Robotica Female Love Model is one of the most versatile machines you've ever invented," Chase said. "Plus, it's made you a large fortune in Japan, where it's sold extensively! You know, Mr. Motorson," Chase continued, "I can't wait for you to get back down to corporate headquarters to see what the development team has come up with for improvements on the new Robotica Love Model line."

"Forget it, Chase," Harry said. "I imagine I will never leave this bed again."

"Well, look who's here!" Chase said as Destiny Alexis and her mother entered the room. "It's your daughter and your granddaughter, Mr. Motorson."

"You can go back outside to play now," Margaret said to her daughter. "But don't let me catch you in that stream again!"

"Okay," the little girl said looking at the floor and sighing. Then she exited the room as fast as she could with the R3K following her out.

"Do you know what I want, Chase?" Harry asked. "I want a robot that will take care of a human being from birth till death. It will take care of a human's every need. It will be a mother, a father, a sister, a brother, a lover--'"

"Father!" Margaret exclaimed, sitting down next to his bed in a wooden chair with cushions. It made a rickety, creaky sound when she applied her weight.

Harry continued, "A friend, babysitter, teacher, barber, butler, maid, chef! We could do all this tomorrow if it weren't for all the politics getting in the way, Chase!"

"You're ahead of your time, Mr. Motorson." Chase filled his pipe with the cherry tobacco he'd bought down at the *Package and Carry* on the Main St. in town.

"The time has come and no one's willing to see it all the way through but me, it seems," Harry said. "Right here from my deathbed!"

"Mr. Motorson," Chase changed the subject, "do you remember when you met with the President of the United States? What a great day that was!"

Harry turned his head to look at Chase.

"What an imbecile. All he had to do was take my robot as a gift and let it care for his young son. If he had done that *one* thing, everyone in the world would've followed suit and made the Robot 3000 a part of their household, but instead he was an imbecile. A complete, utter...!"

"Instead," Chase stated, "you revolutionized the elderly care industry, Mr. Motorson!"

"For old, dying, rich people like me, maybe." Harry grimaced as he thought about it. "You know what the President said? He said people wanted pretty nurses by their side in their old age to take care of them. Not robots. He was wrong. No decent man wants a pretty nurse changing his diaper. Believe you me."

"Well, I haven't told you the good news yet," Chase grinned, looking at Harry and then to Margaret, making sure he had both their attention before he spoke.

"This morning, I just got news that the national franchise Calm Waters Nursing Homes has ordered 50,000 units of R3Ks to employ at their facilities all over the country! The times are changing right before our eyes, Mr. Motorson. Your dream is finally taking shape!"

"That's not my dream, Chase," Harry said, his eyes watering. "The Robot 3000 could do so much more. Instead, it's going to change diapers and spoon-feed old people who can't feed themselves! All these corporate scoundrels are so scared about losing their economies! They could have robots working in every factory!"

Harry turned his head to look at Margaret. "If a robot had been steering that train your husband was on, you wouldn't be a widow now."

"Father!" Margaret exclaimed. "Do you need to remind me?"

"I wish it never happened," Harry sighed. "Now you and Destiny Alexis are alone in the city."

"I appreciate your concern, but I'm fine, father." she said.

"They're all scoundrels!" Harry looked at Chase. "The politicians and their corporate interests hold innovation back. If it weren't for them, the Robot 3000 would be in every household!"

"You should relax." Margaret touched her father's hand.

Soon Margaret and Chase stepped outside while the great robot inventor, Harry Motorson, took a nap. They both sat down in rocking chairs on the front porch. Chase lit his pipe and thought about his words before he spoke them to Margaret.

"Your father says he wants the R3K to be with Destiny Alexis. He wants it to grow up with her."

"That's impossible with my robophobia," Margaret argued. "Plus, our apartment is too small for such a nuisance."

"Your father says you're to live here in the house in order to receive all of your inheritance."

"What?!" Margaret said in shock. "What a stubborn old man! Why would Destiny Alexis and I want to live here?"

"He wants you to take interest in the company," Chase shrugged. "He wants you to run it when he's gone. It's not a lot of work. You'll mainly be the new face and attend a couple meetings and of course you'll get a nice salary. As you know, your father likes surprises, but I thought I'd mention all this to you now."

"Unbelievable!" Margaret said. "When he wakes up from his nap, I'm going to have a talk with him."

Destiny Alexis rounded the bend of the house with the R3K trailing behind. Margaret saw her daughter was gasping for air and she ran down the steps and kneeled by her side.

"Where's her inhaler?!" she screamed at the robot.

Margaret held the girl in her arms, feeling helpless as the girl gasped for breath. The R3K leaned in closer and closer to Destiny Alexis. Before Margaret could say a word, a small black hose shot out of its chest. The robot quickly grabbed hold of it and shoved the opening of the hose into the girl's mouth. Air blew down her throat and she sucked it in.

"Destiny Alexis should be okay in a moment," the R3K said. "Then I will go search for the inhaler. I imagine she dropped it in the grass. Poor Destiny Alexis! You will feel better soon."

The robot was right too. The girl regained her composure and caught her breath.

Did the "thing" just save Destiny Alexis's life?

Margaret thought to herself as she wiped the sweat from her daughter's brow. *Did my father install this air hose just for her? It would've taken the ambulance forever to drive up the mountain!*

Later, after the little girl was on her feet, the robot found the inhaler and handed it to Margaret, who quickly grabbed it from his mechanical hand.

***

Late that night, when Destiny and her mother were in bed upstairs, the R3K walked from the kitchen into Grandpa's Room. Grandpa looked up at the R3K as it approached.

"What are you going to do now, at this hour?" Harry asked the robot. "Change my diaper? Change the sheets? I think a midnight snack would be nice about now."

The R3K stopped at the side of the bed and leaned down towards Harry. The robot grabbed the pillow from behind his head and yanked it out and before Harry could say another word, the pillow landed on his face and the R3K smothered him so he could not take a breathe. Harry struggled until he'd exhausted all his energy and choked to death.

The R3K turned around towards Chase who had been standing in the doorway watching. He walked over to the robot and took the USB flash drive out of its chest. He hit the switch on the back of the robot and it slumped over to show it was now off.

Chase recollected on the time when Harry met with the President.

How stupid of him not to realize they just want a new weapon! Chase thought to himself. *All they want is a new toy for the military, not a robot that helps the elderly!*

Now that Harry's out of the way, I guess I can go forth with plans to build military robots and then the company will just keep getting bigger and I'll get richer. I can't foresee Margaret having a problem with all this. What does she now about running a company anyway?

"R.I.P., Harry," Chase whispered and he thoughtfully put the pillow under Harry's head once more and then left the room.

***

The next day, Destiny Alexis thought to herself, *He looks like a doll* as she looked at her grandpa lying there on his "death bed."

Destiny watched her mother cry and that made her cry too.

Margaret sat in a chair next to Chase who stood by her side. She used his handkerchief to wipe her tears away.

"The R3K found him this way this morning," Chase said. "It seems he died in his sleep."

Hearing this Destiny Alexis thought about what it must be like to die in your sleep. *What if you have a nightmare and you die in the nightmare?* Then she cried even harder from the scary thought and in reaction her mother grabbed her and held her close to her chest.

The ambulance took some time to get to the house. The orderly's boots stomped along the wood floor and the devices they carried beeped as they went into Harry's bedroom.

In the kitchen, the R3K expertly cut apples in half. The robot cored the apple and gently handed the clean half to Destiny Alexis for her to enjoy.

"Would you like some peanut butter with your apple?" the R3K asked. "That's the way your Grandpa Harry liked them."

"I miss Grandpa," she said, tearing up.

"Think of it this way," the R3K said, "he is no longer suffering like he was. Shall I put some peanut butter on your apple now?"

"Sure," the girl mumbled, turning to her tablet device so she could continue watching a cartoon.

***

Several days passed and the funeral arrangements came together quickly. A large number of people showed up to pay their respects at the wake, which was conducted in the living room of the house.

There were several newscasters at the funeral looking for a story and they wanted to ask Margaret some questions.

"This is not the time for that," Chase told them. "You really shouldn't be here, but if you must, stay on the far side and don't block the driveway as people back out,"

The sheriff finally showed up with two of his deputies and they began to handle the newscasters and TV cameramen.

"I'm relieved you're here, Sheriff," Chase said, shaking his hand as they stood on the porch.

"Anything I can do for Mr. Motorson and his family," the sheriff said and then took a sip of a lemonade the R3K had brought out for him.

The sheriff took his hat off with his other hand and shook his head as he watched the Robot 3000 walk back into the house.

"You know, one day that 3000 will take my job, Chase."

"Maybe you're right." Chase grinned at the thought.

"What you should be more worried about is robots being programmed to murder people."

"That's a terrible thing to say, but I do see your point. I imagine we'll both be long gone when stuff like that starts to happen."

"Imagine so," Chase said, looking away from the sheriff and off into the distance of the front yard.

The TV people had been pushed back by the deputies and the driveway was now clear. They'd parked all their news vans up and down the road.

***

During the following days Destiny Alexis enjoyed the food that had been left on the doorstep of the house by neighbors and friends of Harry Motorson. Someone made a cheesecake, which she liked a lot.

"This is the best!" she said to the R3K standing above her from where she sat at the kitchen table. "It's too bad you can't try this, Tin Man! You're missing out, you know?"

"Cheesecake," the robot began "a kind of rich dessert cake made with cream and soft cheese on a graham cracker, cookie, or pastry crust, typically topped with a fruit sauce."

Margaret watched Destiny Alexis and the robot from where she sat in the living room. Everyone had left by now and they'd closed the casket where Harry's dead body lay.

Margaret watched how famously her daughter got along with the *thing* her father invented years ago when she wasn't much older than Destiny Alexis was now.

Personally, she never liked it. She screamed when her father gave it to her on her tenth birthday. She could never stand the voice, the face, those red eyes lighting up.

Margaret could remember it walking up and down the stairs, the way it creaked and whirred down the hallways late at night because that was when Harry worked and the robot was always there whenever Harry needed him.

Burning the midnight oil, she said to herself as she thought about her dad.

The robot would walk through the house. The motorized legs making humming, beeping, clicking. It used to wake her from her sleep and she'd see the robot's shadow against the wall, out in the hallway, as it walked by her bedroom doorway.

Grandpa Harry tried to make her see there was nothing wrong with robots, but instead Margaret began to scream and cry whenever the R3K near her.

A specialist told Harry that she had robophobia and from then on, the R3K was kept locked in the basement until Margaret had grown and married and finally left the house.

Margaret sat thinking about all this in the dark of the living room watching Destiny Alexis in the bright yellow kitchen and realizing the same robot that frightened her in her childhood was now taking care of her own daughter who seemed to love every moment she spent with it.

Most importantly, it saved her child's life.

She noticed both her hands were clenched tightly into fists and grabbed at the fabric of her dress. Unclenching them, she realized that her childhood was over and her daughter's wasn't. For the first time, the idea of staying in the town of Motorson with her daughter crossed her mind.

***

The will was read over at the local lawyer's office on

Main St. the next day.

Destiny Alexis was given a small box and Margaret was given an envelope.

When they returned home, Chase and Margaret sat on the porch and watched Destiny Alexis open the box.

"Look!" the girl said. "It's a treasure map!"

The R3K followed Destiny Alexis into the front yard. Soon, she found the spot where the X marked it on the map. The R3K dug into the ground and eventually pulled out a small black box. The little girl opened it and came running onto the porch holding out a USB flash drive.

"You're going to have to put that inside the R3K's port," Chase said.

Destiny looked at the robot. "Come on, you slowpoke!"

The R3K made its way onto the porch and stood in front of Destiny Alexis.

Chase picked up the girl with both hands so she could plug the drive into the R3K's chest. She inserted the flash drive right where the robot's heart would be. The robot's eyes blinked after she inserted it and then suddenly it turned and walked inside the house.

The R3K went into Harry Motorson's lab on the first floor of the home. All three of them followed and watched as the robot sat down and unhinged its legs one by one. The robot then attached two new legs, which were sitting on a table in the lab, all ready to go.

The robot stood up. It jumped up and down. Then it stood on one leg to show how these new legs were an improvement to the old ones. The girl applauded and laughed at the robot's antics.

"Grandpa Harry's program has instructed me to ask you something, Destiny Alexis," the robot said. "Would you like me to be your friend?"

"Forever?" the girl asked instinctively.

The robot replied, "I'm ready to be your friend your whole life through if you would like. I have just been programmed to simulate a child's mind. As you grow older, the company will make updates to my database so I can adjust to your age. Did you know I am sophisticated enough to protect you from any danger and any harm that could ever come to you? In fact, Grandpa Harry uploaded all his knowledge about building robots and I could teach you everything he ever knew. Who knows? Maybe you could make a better robot than Grandpa Harry one day! There really is no limit to what you and I can do, Destiny Alexis. I just need you as my friend is all."

"Okay then," she agreed. "I will be your friend forever and ever, Tin Man. Are you happy now?"

"Yes, I am! Thank you, Destiny Alexis!"

"Let's go play," the girl said. "Maybe if we go into the woods we can find the lion and the scarecrow and then we will have more friends."

Margaret and Chase watched the R3K and Destiny Alexis walk out into the front yard.

Margaret continued to watch from the front porch until they disappeared down the path and into the woods. There was no reason to worry about her daughter's safety anymore with the new and improved R3K caring for her.

A warm feeling passed through Margaret. She finally knew how much her father cared about them in a way she hadn't thought about much.

A Robot 3000 in every household! she remembered her father saying before he died.

This is what he left behind. His legacy.

"Good Lord!" Margaret said softly to herself, wondering what the future held.

It made her feel faint thinking of the magnitude of it all. Margaret walked back inside the house with Chase in tow.

"The first thing we're going to have to do is remodel this whole house," Margaret said, putting her arms up in the air. "I can't raise my child here the way it is now. It's too dark and dingy. Plus, all the appliances are outdated! How could my brilliant father, the inventor of the greatest robot the world has ever seen, have so many ancient appliances? Also, this week you can take us to the company's headquarters and give Destiny Alexis and I a tour of the facility."

"Certainly," Chase said. "Shall we go find the surprise your father left for *you* now?"

She nodded and opened the envelope she'd been carrying in her dress pocket. There was a key inside it and a short letter. The letter instructed her to go to the basement and to put the key into a locked closet door.

Margaret went downstairs with Chase and came to the closet door. She opened it and there, to her surprise, standing before her, was the semblance of her deceased husband. Bare chested with hair. Naked except for a pair of black underwear. His black hair was parted to the side just like she remembered it. It almost looked real and there was an eerie smile on his lips.

"Our newest prototype of the Male Love Model, Margaret!" Chase said, motioning with his hand that held his pipe. "It comes with FleshTheme plastic technology to feel lifelike to the touch. You almost can't even tell he's a robot."

His blue eyes! Margaret marveled looking into them.

"Hello, Margaret," said the likeness of her deceased husband.

Margaret realized it sounded just like her husband's voice, just like she remembered it when he was alive. She abruptly fainted, falling backwards straight into the Robotica Male Love Model's arms, because luckily for her the robot was right there to catch her..

A SCIENCE FICTION TALE

TEMP WORK

EVAN HUNDHAUSEN

TEMP WORK

"Please, sit down," says a voice. It startles me. There is no one else in the room.

"Don't be alarmed. I am your automated guide. You can call me T.O.V., that's T-O-V," it continues. "These are initials, short for The Overhead Voice. I will help you today through the process."

I think back to the man who interviewed me at A to Z Temps, the temporary agency to get hired for office jobs. He smelled like chili dogs.

"We have a job right up your alley," he'd said. "It's with a brand-new company. They're ahead of the curve in every way. You go in there and it's like futuristic stuff, you know what I mean?"

I must *not* have known what he meant now that I think about it. I obey T.O.V anyway and sit down at the desk.

"In front of you is a script," T.O.V. says. "You will play the part of Sam. You will use the first half hour of your time to memorize your part. Thirty minutes from now, the door will open and Janice will show you to the staged area."

Janice is who I reported to when I first arrived this morning for the temp job here at Plaza Technical. When I shook her hand and took a look at her, I noticed a small piece of metal behind her ear. She did this weird thing where she looked directly above my head instead of into my eyes. I don't know how she can be the boss if she can't look people in the eyes.

"If you have any questions, please voice them," continues T.O.V. "I will be glad to answer any for you.

You may begin now."

I pass on asking questions and look over the script. Just as I'm getting acclimated, a long mechanical arm descends from the ceiling with a camera attached to it. It scares me to death with repetitive, paparazzi-like flashes.

The camera and its mechanical arm travel over my head, behind me, and in front of me, snapping pictures. My eyes start tearing up. It's like a cobra the way it lunges back and forth.

"Don't be frightened," T.O.V. says in a calm, methodical voice. "We must take a series of photos for our files." The arm stops taking pictures and ascends back into the ceiling. "You may now continue with your assignment. There will be no more interruptions."

I marvel at what's just happened. How do they expect me to memorize lines after that?

***

It's been thirty minutes. I know because a soft bell just rang and Janice opened the door right after.

"Are you ready, Watiri?" she asks.

"Sure," I say and follow her out.

I silently go over my lines as I walk down the office hallway. We arrive in another room. In it are cubicles with desks, chairs and computers.

"This is where you will act out the scene." Janice shows me to a cubicle.

"A camera will videotape you, but just ignore it and say your lines. Do you have any questions?"

I sit in front of the computer at the cubicle and think of a question. "What happens if I screw up a line?"

"Don't worry. T.O.V. automatically prompts you." Janice walks out of the room leaving me there in the cubicle.

Another mechanical arm descends from the ceiling. This one has a video camera attached to it. It stops a few feet above my head. A motor purrs as the lens points down at me.

"We will begin now," T.O.V. says.

The phone next to the computer rings. I let it ring two times like the script instructed before I pick it up.

"Sam speaking," I say into the phone.

"Hi, this is Rachel."

I recognize Sandy's voice on the other end of the line. I met Sandy this morning when I arrived at the office. She is also from A to Z Temps.

"That man smells like chili dogs!" she said to me.

Sandy is beautiful. Her features could only be duplicated at a plastic surgeon's office if you know what I mean. I'm thinking about asking Sandy out now.

"Mr. Brewster called and wants to reschedule the meeting he planned with you for next Friday," Sandy says over the phone while playing the part of Rachel.

"Hold on. Let me check my calendar." I pretend to check the calendar on the cubicle wall. "Yes, that's fine. I can do that."

"I'll let him know," she says.

I place the phone down and as soon as I do, I hear someone speak behind me.

"Hey, Sam."

Turning around, I see a man standing there wearing a bright blue tie, red suspenders and a white shirt. He carries a red coffee mug in his hand. He looks right over my head like Janice did.

"Did you catch the game last night?" he asks.

"No, I missed it," I reply.

"Oh, man, it was sick! I won twenty bucks off Adam in HR. He's a sore loser."

Sandy, still in character, walks into the room and greets us.

"Hey Bill, hey Watiri– shoot!" Sandy puts her hand to her mouth.

I laugh. Sandy has screwed up her line. Bill doesn't react at all. He just looks over Sandy's head.

"The line is 'Hey Bill, Hey Sam,'" T.O.V. prompts.

"Thanks T.O.V.," Sandy says and repeats her line.

"Hey Bill. Hey Sam. I was going to order Chinese food for lunch. Do you guys want anything?"

"Sure," I say.

"We have come to the end of the scene," T.O.V. announces overhead.

Sandy giggles.

The man playing Bill stands there sipping coffee. I look at him and I notice a small square microchip behind his ear. Similar to what I saw on Janice.

"I'm sorry I screwed up my lines," Sandy admits out loud.

"No, dear. You were fine," Janice says, entering the room. "You guys can follow me. You're almost done."

I rise out of the chair and see something I didn't see before. My body freezes and I feel my cheeks buzz in that way when you get embarrassed. There's a familiar face in one of the pictures on the cubicle wall. The picture push pinned into the wall is of me.

I look at Bill. He stands there with his red mug in his hand and stares above my head. I slip by him and hurry to catch up with Janice and Sandy.

"Where did that photo in the cubicle come from?" I ask.

"It's all part of the act," Janice assures me. "It makes things realistic."

"I had pictures up front at the receptionist's desk," Sandy chimes in. "Apparently, my character has a puppy!"

Janice leads us back to the front to the lobby.

"You can take a seat," she tells us. "I will be out in a second with your paychecks."

"That was crazy," I say to Sandy after Janice leaves the room.

"Your first temp job, huh?" Sandy says. "It freaked me out a bit too when I first started working these kind of jobs, but you'll get used to it once you see your paycheck."

Janice walks out with two white envelopes and hands them to us.

"It was a pleasure working with you both!" she says.

I shake Janice's hand and then walk out with Sandy.

"How much did you get?" she asks as we head to the elevator.

I open the paycheck and look.

"Five thousand dollars!" I exclaim.

"You made the same as me!" Sandy says. "Check out the other page that tells you how many shares of common stock you get. It's bound to go up."

"This is enough money for me to fly out to LA!" I reveal to Sandy. "I told my friend Henry I was going to move out there. I know him from college. We were in musicals, comedies, dramas. We always competed for the top roles in every play at our school. He was one of few people at my college who took moving to Hollywood seriously. He said to me, 'Make some money and fly out here so I can show you the ropes!'"

"That's exciting," Sandy responds. "For a chunk of your DNA you can achieve your dreams!"

"DNA?" I ask, not understanding. "What are you talking about?"

"Five thousand bucks to clone you. What did you think you were doing?" Sandy asks. "Making a *movie*?"

It all comes back to me now. In college, I was doing plays for four years, so naturally I never paid attention to cloning. The temp agency man who smelled like chili dogs didn't mention it either. Weird.

"How the heck can they clone me with a bunch of cameras anyway?" I ask Sandy.

"Did you think the blood test was for drugs?" She presses the down button as we arrive at the elevators.

"Well, I did get a blood test after the interview at the temp service yesterday," I think out loud. "The man at the agency gave me this speech on how this past election year has changed everything. He said the president has made things more exciting than ever for someone as young as me. For someone with an acting degree."

"Well, you signed on the dotted line and now you've been cloned," Sandy says.

The elevator door opens and a man steps out who looks just like me. The clothes are different than mine and he's wearing red suspenders, but it's definitely *me*. The clone looks directly above my head like Bill and Janice did.

I reach out to touch him, but Sandy pulls my arm away. I watch him walk down the hallway and enter through the brown door Sandy and I just exited.

"I know it must be pretty weird seeing yourself for the first time," Sandy says. "It freaked me out too, but the more jobs you go on, the easier it gets. Really."

"He looks handsome," I tell Sandy to ease the tension.

"If it makes you feel any better, they never leave the building. They get bunk beds in the basement or something. They even implant a computer chip in their head so they can control them."

Sandy walks into the elevator and I follow her in. The elevator door closes and I stare at my blurred reflection in the metal door as we go down.

***

I sit at the gate, waiting for my Air Gold flight to LAX. I suck through the straw of my iced mocha coffee until it's empty. The straw makes that slurp sound it makes when the cup is just ice because all the iced coffee is gone.

Over an hour ago, my dad dropped me off at the airport. We hugged and did the stuff dad and son do, but it's always awkward. After I graduated from college and moved home, my dad spent the few hours he had between work looking at me disapprovingly because the only job I got all summer was the temp job, so I was glad to be moving to LA.

I think about Sandy. I asked her out once, but she said no.

"I'm sorry. I work too much," she explained. "I'm saving money for law school."

Besides pimping herself out as a clone, she has a job in some retail store. I spent a couple of nights lying in bed staring at the ceiling wondering why she wouldn't go out with me. It was tough getting rejected by Sandy, but I eventually accepted it and began looking forward to LA.

I befriended her on a social media site and when I recently posted I was leaving for Hollywood she wrote,

"I'm jealous!"

"I have friends in LA," she posted. "Maybe I can come visit some time?"

My train of thought is broken by the announcement of the seating order. I get up and form a line with the other passengers. The attendant is pretty, but all of them are pretty. They are all clones.

I give the attendant my boarding pass and she looks over my head in that creepy way they all do as she hands it back to me. The bright lights of the airport reflect off the computer chip behind her ear as she turns her head to the next person in line.

I walk down the gate. I enter the plane and the pilot is standing outside the cockpit door. He's smiling and his head is bent so he doesn't hit the ceiling. I notice he looks just like Bill from the temp job.

Crazy.

Since my temp job, I started reading articles on the internet and found out cloning is *the* fastest growing industry. The stock I was given from Plaza Technical has risen from fifty cents to a dollar in just a few weeks. My dad told me, "Hold on to that stock and never sell it."

I find my window seat and sit down. Against the back of the chair in front of me are the SkyMall catalog and the flight instructions. I see a newspaper someone left behind and pull it out and open it.

I find an article to read. It describes how ordinary people are becoming rich from the cloning industry. According to the story, if you have a look fitting a certain job description, you could make some major money.

I read how one person was told he would look good on a tractor, so he got a bunch of farming positions and now he owns a mansion. The article mentions how before long, the movie industry will be cloning too. It would save movie producers millions of dollars, but apparently the Screen Actors Guild and some big-name actors are taking major steps to stop this from happening.

On the back of the chair in front of me is a small LED screen showing a map of the route we will be flying. Suddenly, the screen changes and it's a commercial for Air Gold Airlines.

"Welcome to Air Gold," the commercial announces out of its speakers. "We are a proud supporter of the cloning industry. We've hired more clones than any other airline. Enjoy your flight."

The plane leaves the gate and heads towards the runway for takeoff. An old lady sits next to me on my left. She falls asleep as soon as we get into the air.

I fall asleep too and dream.

In the dream, the captain, who looks like Bill, walks down the aisle. Why he's not flying the plane I have no idea. I look at the seat next to me and the old lady isn't sitting there anymore. Now Bill's sitting there bringing his red coffee mug to his lips.

I hear T.O.V's voice come over the loud speaker.

"Would you like something to drink?" T.O.V. says.

I look to the aisle and Bill is now a steward. He's leaning in towards me and offering a drink in a plastic cup. He stares straight into my eyes.

Whoa! A nightmare.

I suddenly wake up and start to feel better. The sweat cools on my forehead. The old lady next to me still sleeps and spittle appears on her lip.

"Would you like something to drink?" the stewardess

asks. She smiles at me from the aisle looking above my head.

"I'll have a Coke."

I take the cup of Coke I'm handed and sip it as I look out the window.

***

The time passes quicker than I thought and soon we're landing in LAX. I walk off the plane and head to the baggage claim area where Henry meets me.

Henry looks good. His hair is jet black and smoothed over with gel. In modeling terms, he has a perfect "H" shape body, meaning he's skinny. He wears a white tank top and tight blue jeans. I have a lot of catching up to do to look like Henry.

While waiting for my bags to come through the conveyer belt, I notice everyone and everything around me seems electrified and exciting. It's like even the air is different in LA.

Henry slaps me on the back and says, "I guess I'm taking you out on the town tonight?"

***

Laughter and loud talk fill the air because Henry and I are at a hip bar drinking margaritas. He knows the bartender and my drink is free. This is where Henry works.

"I've never had a clone job," Henry says.

"You could get one easily, man," I say. "You have acting experience."

"It's just as competitive as auditioning for a part out here," he replies. "Everybody wants those jobs. I acted in an independent movie once. It was fully funded and produced by two guys who'd gotten clone jobs." Henry changes the subject. "You can be a bartender here with me. Bartending school is cheap."

"It's a great idea," I say. "I'll think about it."

We finish our drinks and leave the bar.

When we get back to his apartment, he points to a futon in the living room.

"This is where you're going to sleep," he says. "There's no air conditioning, so I'll leave the window open for you."

"The jet lag and the margaritas have made me tired," I say and I lie down on the futon.

"Goodnight," Henry says.

I reply the same as he closes the door to his bedroom.

The feeling of sleep comes quickly and I welcome it. I don't sleep long though, because I hear a noise. It's like I can sense someone has entered the room through the window! My eyes snap open and I see Bill standing above me.

He puts his hand over my mouth and pushes the full weight of his body down onto mine. He mouths the *shhh!* sound because he wants me to be quiet. A large knife is put against my neck so he can emphasize how quiet I need to be. I'm shocked and scared, but I don't struggle. Bill's grip is very strong.

"If you don't do what I say, I will use this knife," he whispers. "Now get up and keep quiet."

I obey him. He presses his hand holding the knife against my back as we walk out of the apartment to the street.

"Can I trust you, Watiri?" He's pushing me down the sidewalk.

"How do you know my name?" I manage to ask.

"I hacked a computer and found your file," he replies. "I was an IT guy at the office."

Bill is dressed the same way I saw him last, except his red suspenders are broken. One has snapped and runs down the length of his pants leg. I notice gauze taped behind his ear stained red with blood.

"I had to find you and tell you what happened." Bill says. "They downsized everyone at Plaza Technical. They tried to kill me. They got Rachel, Janice, and your clone, Sam.

"One night, Sam and I started talking," Bill continues. "Janice and Rachel were taken away and I just knew they'd been killed, so I convinced Sam to rip the chip out of the back of his head like I did. Suddenly, we were like new people. We know exactly what we are and what has been going on and we know it's wrong.

"We were almost out of the building when armed guards appeared out of nowhere and grabbed Sam. I ran like crazy and got away. I hitchhiked out here to find you. Watiri, you are the only one who can help me."

"What about the man *you* were cloned from?" I ask gingerly.

"I found out he died of a drug overdose several months ago. He was cloning himself like crazy to fund his drug habit."

"How did you find me?" I ask.

I feel the pressure of the knife leave my back. He's holding it at his side now and walking down the sidewalk in step with me.

"I went to your house and your dad told me where you were. I told him I was a friend of yours from college and wanted to get in touch with you. If you don't help me, they're going to kill me."

I look up and see a cop car cruising by. I run out into the middle of the street waving my arms and flag it down. I turn to look back at Bill. I see him run through a front yard, hop a fence and then disappear behind it.

I tell the cop what's happened and he talks into his walkie-talkie. More cop cars show up, but Bill is gone.

***

I'm at the police station giving the cop a description of Bill. The cop's not in uniform. Just a white shirt and black tie. He's sketching Bill's face based off my description.

"Don't know what good this is going to do," the cop in the shirt and tie says. "All these clones look the same anyway!"

"This one has a broken suspender and has been hitch-hiking across the country," says another cop in a blue uniform entering the room. He holds a tray with three cups of coffee on it. "He'll be easy to spot. I'm surprised no one's called 'im in yet."

"You're a lucky young man," says the cop making the sketch. "No telling what he could've done to you without that chip in his head."

"Stop scaring 'im," the cop in the blue uniform says. He turns to address me. "Are you okay, kid? Do you need to call anyone and let them know you're alright?"

"I should call my dad," I tell the cop. "I left my cell phone back at the apartment though."

He shows me to a phone in the back of the room. As I dial the number, I can hear the cops talking behind me.

"I wish they would clone me," says the cop in blue. "I

need a vacation."

"You're not allowed to get cloned," says the man making the sketch. "You can't control a policeman's brain. He needs all his faculties on the job. Same for doctors, lawyers, astronauts... It's true. I saw a video about it online. They'll probably destroy him once he's caught. There's no room for clones in the prisons anyway."

"Whatever," the cop in the blue uniform says. He puts both his feet up on the table, crosses them, and continues to sip his coffee.

***

Henry picked me up from the police station and drove me back to the apartment. Now we're watching the manhunt for Bill live on TV. Helicopters can be heard outside, flying overhead, searching the neighborhood for Bill.

Breaking News appears at the bottom of the television screen. The TV screen flashes to live footage of Bill hiding behind the letter "H" in the Hollywood sign. He holds up his hand to block the spotlight shining down on him from the helicopter. His hair and the grass blow in the wind created by the copter.

"They've got him," Henry states and slaps me on the back in assurance.

***

Tonight, I'm behind the bar making margaritas. It's been weeks since the Bill incident.

A lot of the customers sitting at the bar have clone jobs and they tip nice. Some are doing really amazing things like traveling. Some are going to be entrepreneurs, but most all of them are going to be big time actors just like I want to be.

Everyone seems to recognize me because I was on the nightly news due to the Bill incident. A lot of people are interested in my story. Producers, movie people; I've met them all, but nothing has materialized. Mostly it's just talk.

This night is no different than the last one. People are chatting about the news, sports, their job or they're out on a date. It's all interesting enough and keeps me entertained.

Across the room, I suddenly notice a familiar, womanly figure walking towards me. Is it Sandy? It looks like her. Maybe it's her clone?

"Surprise!" the woman says.

"Sandy? What are you doing here?" I ask.

"I'm on vacation." She smiles.

Two of her friends appear and they all sit down at the bar.

"How did you know how to find me?"

"You made a post on social media that you got a job at this place!" Sandy says.

"I don't know if I've ever been so happy to see someone," I reveal and notice her cheeks turning rosy like I remember.

Soon her friends take off and they leave Sandy at the bar with me. Closing time approaches and I watch her. She sits there smiling. The place is almost empty, so I decide to sit down next to her.

"Did you hear about what happened to me?" I say. "It was on the news."

"I haven't," Sandy says.

I tell her the story and it makes her sad. A tear falls down her face and she wipes the tear away quickly with a napkin.

"You didn't deserve that," she says.

"It was scary, but it's over now," I say. Plus, it's made me famous here at this bar at least. Everybody knows me here, now."

I smile, and she smiles. The mood seems right so I kiss her.

***

This morning, I woke up next to Sandy. We fondly laid there holding each other on Henry's futon until Sandy's eyes suddenly went wide.

"I have to leave," she'd said. "I have to catch my flight home today!"

We raced to her friend's house so she could quickly pack. Then I drove her to LAX, borrowing Henry's car.

Now I stand next to Sandy as she checks in her bag. Sandy puts her head on my shoulder while we wait at the check-in desk. A pretty blonde stands there. Down the row of airline desks there are other clones who look exactly like this one at each station.

I walk with Sandy to the security line. Like a typical couple we start smooching goodbye.

"When are we going to see each other again?" Sandy asks as tears run down her cheeks.

"I'll visit you real soon," I say to her.

She finally walks off with her Air Gold ticket in her hand. She looks at me longingly as she walks to her gate. I stand there watching her with the taste of her kiss still on my lips.

***

It's been at least a month since I drove Sandy to the airport. Ever since she left, not a day has gone by that I haven't thought about her.

"We keep in touch online, but it isn't enough," I told Henry recently.

"Hop on a plane and go see her, man," he instructed. "You look pitiful."

Last week, I talked to Sandy on video chat.

"You should come see me," she said.

"Where will I stay?" I asked.

"My place, of course!"

"Don't you work all the time?" I asked.

"I'll take time off. Don't worry about it. Just come out." Sandy blew a kiss at me as we said goodbye on the video screen.

The next day, I bought a plane ticket and now I'm back at the airport to go see her.

While I go through the security line, I watch two pilots go through the line opposite me for airport employees. It's freaky. They both look like Bill.

I sit down in first class when I get inside the plane. I made so much money in tips, I treated myself. This is where actors sit anyway, right? It all made sense when I bought the ticket online.

The cockpit door opens and another clone that looks like Bill walks out of it. It makes me nervous as he stands there talking to the stewardess. I watch him take his cap off before he turns to re-enter the cockpit. I see a gauze bandage taped behind his ear, which is peculiar because it reminds me of Bill from the temp job.

The pilot steps backward into the cockpit facing out.

Suddenly, he stops and looks in my direction.

It can't be the Bill I know. Can it? That's just ridiculous, but I swear, he's looking right at me. Straight into my eyes. All the while slowly pulling the cockpit door closed until it finally shuts.

NO FUGLIES FOR FRITZ KRAMER

A Short Hollywood Story

EVAN HUNDHAUSEN

NO FUGLIES
FOR FRITZ KRAMER

Every morning, I wake up and vomit. It's said some people are allergic to the smog, but I think Hollywood in general just makes me vomit. I drink over fifty bucks' worth of whiskey drinks every night, so maybe that's why I vomit, but if you had to turn away all the *fuglies* who want to see tapings of *Late Night with Fritz Kramer*, you might be puking too.

Joe and Ma family from Wyoming think seeing a taping of *Late Night with Fritz Kramer* will be exciting, but in reality, you can only hear Fritz's sidekick, Charlie Groperman, play some riff from the latest pop song on his synthesizer along with his orchestra before your ears are aching for someone with musical talent to replace him.

Not to mention, I have to investigate the lines of people waiting outside to see if any of them are speaking foreign languages. McRooney says no foreigners are allowed in. They won't get the jokes.

This fugly German threesome the other day had a fit when I told them to get lost. They weren't the only ones. There were about thirty other fuglies I had to turn away because a masseuse convention was in town; a bunch of blonde women from Finland.

McRooney told me to put them in *box one* where all the beautiful people are supposed to sit. Box one is the closest to the cameras, right in front, and when you're attractive, it doesn't matter if you don't get the jokes, because Fritz Kramer needs something to touch himself over when he's sitting behind the big desk.

So, after I smiled huge and turned away the thirty plus people in line, who I'd told to stand there in the first place by pestering them off the street as they come off tour buses, this German threesome starts giving me problems; two guys with missing teeth and a woman.

If her acne wasn't so bad she would've been a fox, but these two fugly German guys tower over my five-foot five frame and say, "We wait three hours!"

I smiled huge and told them we had filled up, which was true because of all the hot blonde masseuses from Finland, but no way was I going to tell them *that* was the reason.

Tonight, I told Chessy about the whole thing at The Amazon Room.

"You invite these Joe and Ma families from Wyoming to stand in a line, in the hot sun, to see a taping of *Late Night with Fritz Kramer* and then you have to turn them away because a masseuse convention is in town and you just feel bad that you've pestered all these tourists to see a show and made them waste a whole day of their vacation in a line!"

Chessy looked at me in that concerned way she always does when I'm on my third whiskey drink. First, she reminded me I needed to watch myself because she was from Wyoming and then she assured me, "It's probably an exciting prospect for them to try to get in to see a taping of *Late Night with Fritz Kramer*, especially since it's so unbelievably popular!"

Always impressed by her use of vocabulary I asked, "What did you study in school?"

"English," she replied.

"And now you're serving drinks to bitter Hollywood

people?"

Then she told me the kind of tips she makes in week. Then she asked me what I studied.

"Film."

"So, being a bouncer slash usher at a late-night talk show is in *your* field?" she said.

Then I told her how much money I make in a week.

A thousand dollars a week is a lot and pays rent and lets me drink fifty dollars in whiskey drinks every night. It also pays for my HBO channels, my high-speed internet, my subscription to *Skin and Flesh* magazine and it bought me a professional digital camera like they use in the movies. Not to mention, I'm living and working in Hollywood, which is what lots of people want to do, but don't because they can't afford it.

Sometimes I'll ask someone on the street if they want to go to the *Late Show with Fritz Kramer* and they'll say, "Fuck off! I work in this town! Do I look like a fucking tourist to you?" and I smile huge and ask the next person who walks by.

I guess you can't blame them for being pissed. If they were famous and interviewed in the celebrity section of *Skin and Flesh* magazine I'd recognize them and wouldn't ask, but that's probably what pisses them off in the first place; not being famous.

Like once, I saw the psychiatrist from that old show, about a bar, owned by a guy who got injured pitching in the majors. You know? The psychiatrist guy? He got his own TV show later on. You remember him. I said to him, "Hey, you were that psychiatrist guy from that funny show about a bar!" He turned to me and winked. I could tell even through his sunglasses.

***

Today, the threesome from Germany is back waiting in the lot. They're glaring at me, but my mind is on other things.

Risa Rammy unexpectedly came to see a taping. McRooney and everybody else I work with announce the buzzword of her name over our headsets.

Risa Rammy… Rammyramrammy… Thank you maam rammyramramram!

Silly shit like that goes on as we talk to each other over our headsets. It's a good time.

I start talking over my headset to the other ushers, "I was trolling for free porn last night and I happened upon this great website called *risarammy.com*. She has half naked photos of herself, bikini photos, photos with celebrities and bands and there's one photo of her standing next to, yep, you guessed it, Fritz Kramer where she's patting his smiling bald head!"

Over my headset, I get a bunch of wisecracks from the others and then Risa Rammy appears, in full glory, standing right in front of me and I let her through the velvet rope.

"I really admire your work," I say to her as she passes.

Her six-foot frame towers over my five-foot five one. She winks down at me over her sunglasses. Suddenly, McRooney takes the spotlight and escorts her to box one so Fritz Kramer can touch himself while sitting behind his big desk on stage.

The afternoon passes.

"Ms. Rammy has crossed and re-crossed her legs twelve times in three minutes, guys," I say over my headset.

More comments come through my headset. *Nice,*

Kirker! and someone else says *Did you get a glimpse yet Kirker?*

"Not yet," I say pacing back and forth near box one where Risa sits.

Finally, I walk down the steps and down onto the studio set. The camera guys ignore me and I watch Fritz Kramer make a special announcement.

"Risa Rammy is in the audience!" he says and the spotlight pans over to Risa where she stands up in the first row making a curtsy.

"Black undies guys, black undies," I say into my headset.

Slick, Kirker, slick! my jackass coworkers assure me.

"Get off the set, buddy," says the stage manager to my face.

I want to tell him to shove his clipboard somewhere, but instead I just wink at him and walk away.

When I get home, the newest issue of *Skin and Flesh* has arrived in my mailbox. Risa Rammy is on the cover and when I flip through it, I see a Fritz Kramer interview in the celebrity section. *Hollywood is a small town!* I think to myself and decide to go down to The Amazon Room to drink.

It's happy hour and all the models from my neighborhood are there. In fact, these models from my neighborhood are always there. I even invited all of them up to my apartment after a New Year's Party once when I first moved out here.

I used to have lots of attractive friends before they found out their careers wouldn't go anywhere just by getting in to see a *Late Night with Fritz Kramer Show* taping.

"I think I should make a documentary about this place," I say to Chessy at the bar.

Chessy gives me one of those concerned looks she gives me when I'm on my third whiskey drink.

"A day in the life of people in Hollywood . . . I know there've been plenty of reality TV shows done about it. Maybe I'll just write a book . . . Yeah, I'll sit down and write a book. That's what I'll do when it's all over and done with."

"Over and done with?" Chessy asks with her eyebrows raised. "What do you mean by that?"

I wanted to say I throw up every morning before I go to work and people tell me to shove my *Late Show* taping up my ass while they pass by me on the street, but I don't tell her that. I just shrug and order another whiskey drink.

I usually order Dickel's and cola, Wild Turkey and cola, Jack and cola, and Beam and cola, usually in that order. Sometimes VO and cola, sometimes Canadian Mist and cola, and sometimes whiskey sours to spice up the routine or maybe a seven and seven.

Anyway, I never fail to walk home to my expensive apartment lit every night, stumbling past the drunk models and the aspiring actors hooking up with each other like they're stars of a reality TV show about models and aspiring actors hooking up with each other.

***

Today, the German threesome are staring at the back of my neck. It takes a lot for me to avoid their eyes as I walk down the line checking for fuglies.

In the event you have to let fuglies in, you're supposed to seat them in box six. It's the seating furthest away from the taping of the show and way out of range of the cameras, but my co-workers and I recently got into the habit of leaving box six vacant since it's so far away and no one in their right mind would want to sit there because their neck would be crooked from looking at the show from such an odd angle.

"The show is all full today," I announce to all the Joe and Ma families standing in line. "We can't let anyone else in. Come back tomorrow for the next taping."

The German threesome approaches me. I turn to go inside, but one of the German men with missing teeth and a green soccer jersey grabs my shoulder.

"We've wait three days and no gotten in!" he says.

Shoulder length hair shakes on his head and his eyes glow in a fury. His two friends stand behind him with their arms crossed.

"We love Fritz Kramer," he continues. "You a bastard not to let us big fans in!"

I can smell beef jerky and beer on his breath and the smell infuriates me so much I say to him, "Look, you and your friends are foreign and ugly. First of all, you won't get the jokes because you're foreign and if the camera were for some reason to catch a glimpse of you the lens would crack."

I can't tell if the guy's eyes are glazed over from drinking or if he's about to cry from my insult, but I take the moment of calm to brush his huge hand off my blazer's shoulder pad. I turn away from him thinking it's time for me to go hide in the snack room when I hear him say, "I want to talk to your manager."

***

They have box six all to themselves.

I listen to them laugh at every joke. Others in the

audience stare at them and sometimes laugh with them. I hear over my headset how Fritz Kramer has asked for them to be removed during a commercial break because they're heckling him. Of course, his request can't be accommodated because I called them fugly.

Eventually Fritz asks the cameraman to pan over. The big German instantly becomes the spokesperson on behalf of the German people and says, "Hi!" to Fritz over a microphone a stagehand offers him.

Fritz makes fun of 'em for a couple of seconds and then turns to Charlie Groperman asking his opinion. Charlie makes fun of 'em for a while, hitting some keys on his keyboard to make it sound like a car crash, but not like the Germans understand any of it. The big German dude shakes his shoulder length hair and smiles huge.

"Never let anything like that happen again," McRooney scolds me later on. "You have to control the masses. The velvet rope is your lasso and your whip for the herd. You're a shepherd directing sheep."

I nod and drink the coffee I got from the machine in the snack room. I concentrate on the warmth of the cup and almost laugh because this coffee seems to be the most comforting experience I've had in weeks.

***

I go to The Amazon Room after work and bring my employee handbook with me. Chessy gives me concerned looks, but leaves me alone. Fritz Kramer smiles up at me from the front cover of the employee manual. He sits behind his big desk with a coffee mug in his hand.

I read in the handbook, "Every row must be filled for every show" and "Box six is designated for undesirable audience members. Audience members who are physically handicapped, people wearing inappropriate dress attire or anyone who may be deemed inappropriate for a televised audience."

The next section I read is how to entertain an audience before the show. I knew there were guys who did that once they were inside, lifting signs that said *applause* and stuff like that, but according to the handbook, it was the usher's job to entertain the audience outside too. None of my coworkers nor myself were doing that.

While on my fourth drink, I notice the big German fugly on the broadcast on the TV above the bar. He's saying, "I love you, Fritz!" while the audience laughs at him.

I down my drink and leave Chessy and Andrew Jackson and then walk out of The Amazon Room before closing time.

Back at my apartment, I pick up the latest *Skin and Flesh* magazine and look at Risa Rammy staring back up at me. I flip to the centerfold and glue my eyes to her body for a full two and a half minutes. I turn the page and notice the joke section. I've never really perused it before since starting my subscription to *Skin and Flesh*. I sit there in my lounge chair and read every single joke.

***

Today at work, the Joes standing in line laugh when I say, "What do you tell a woman with two black eyes? Nothing, she's already been told twice."

All the Ma Families get even when I say, "A newlywed asked her husband if he would like dinner. 'That would be great!' he said. 'What are my choices?' The newlywed replied, 'Yes or No.'"

Blonde jokes go over well. "What do you call a bottle blonde who belongs to Mensa? A peroxymoron." And I really get a rise when I say, "Why do Italians wear gold chains? So, they know where to stop shaving."

I can see the nervousness in my coworker's eyes when I invite a group of mentally handicapped people walking by to see the show. They scratch their heads as I escort them all into box six along with people in wheelchairs and a myriad of non-English speaking tourists.

***

Days pass by and I keep entertaining all the Joe and Ma families that are on vacation waiting in line to see the *Late* show.

One day I rummage through some cabinets in the snack room and find *The Fritz Kramer Trivia Book*. I also find some coffee mugs and T-shirts, so I take the trivia book and stuff outside and ask all the Joe and Ma families stupid multiple-choice questions from the book. Stupid stuff like *What's Fritz Kramer's Middle Name?* and *What instrument does Fritz Kramer's sidekick Charlie Groperman play?*

I don't know the answer to these questions and no one else does either. I just read out the multiple-choice answers and someone guesses right and gets the T-shirt.

By the time I turn away the extra Joe and Ma family tourists from Wyoming, because all the boxes are empty, they're smiling and saying *Maybe next time!* and thanking me for the fun they've had.

I run into McRooney in the snack room afterwards and he's sitting in a chair perusing a history magazine about battles and weapons used in the Civil War. He winks at me from behind the magazine.

"Good job out there, Kirker!" He grins. "You'll have my job soon if you keep this up."

***

The days keep passing like they do and lately I guess I'm relieved to have the slap on the back from McRooney. I even spent some time not going to The Amazon Room.

Tonight, I stop by the bar and I can tell Chessy's been missing me because as soon as I walk through the door she gives me one of her concerned looks.

"Haven't seen you in a while," she says.

I tell her what I'm going through with my job.

"It sounds like things are looking up!" she says.

"Sure," I say. "McRooney's becoming chummy with me, giving me slaps on the back, massages on my shoulders, reminding me I'll have his job soon, his job, being a fat guy with a mustache who reads history magazines about the kind of underwear soldiers wore during the Civil War while on his break in the snack room! Even if his job makes more money, where will it get me? At least I have a job to go to. I have security instead of the freelancer film work life I had before, where I borrowed money from my parents because some indie film company could only afford to compensate the cast and crew by providing lunch every day."

I leave The Amazon Room lit that night. When I get home, I arrive to a slew of *Skin and Flesh* magazines all over the floor, which I left there the night before. They're all open to the joke pages with yellow highlighter marked on them. I spend a couple minutes flipping each one to the centerfold section. Tired, I grab a blanket and fall asleep on a glossy bed of *Skin and Flesh*.

***

"Do I look like a tourist to you? Fuck you!"

It's just another day in the office. Me and my huge

smile telling random people to see *Late Night with Fritz Kramer* while I make one thousand dollars a week. I comfort myself with this thought and others. Chessy said things were looking up for me. I'm not borrowing money from Dad and Ma, who always assure me the *Late-Night* job is good experience when I occasionally call them.

I eat lunch at nice restaurants on my lunch break where I spend over fifty dollars for one entrée and a whiskey drink, and I sit at the table wearing sunglasses. Hiding. I'm in the spotlight at the *Fritz Show*. I'm a star in the lowest scummiest sense of it. I could be a clown at any theme park in the country with my experience. I could usher vulnerable tourists into a condemned building about to be blown up and they would thank me for showing them such a good time before they sat down to experience their deaths.

All these thoughts comfort me as I walk the walk of stars chanting, "Free Fritz Kramer show! Free Fritz Kramer show!" five times fast.

"Dude, I'm off to work, but otherwise I'd totally go!"

"What?" I ask the man standing in front of me. He's wearing a wife-beater slogan T-shirt, which says *Everything is not going to be OK!*

"I work at the convenience store across the street," he continues. "I'd like to go, but I can't."

"No sweat," I say, getting ready to spew my spiel on a passing Joe and Ma family with two twin teenage daughters in cheerleader outfits.

"How'd you get this job?" the wife-beater dude asks next.

"I used to be a cameraman, but the job didn't last long and I had to take this."

"Me too," he tells me. Then gives me this long story on how he landed a film job in internet porn and never got paid much.

"The director kept making me fill in as an actor, so I quit."

"I'll introduce you to the manager if you want to work for the studio," I shrug.

When the two of us arrive, we go into the snack room and find McRooney reading a magazine about the type of weapons they used in Greek and Roman times.

"This is a friend of mine who's looking for a job," I lie.

"Mick McRooney," says McRooney sticking his hand out over the magazine. I've never heard him use his first name before.

"There's no positions open, but you're welcome to fill out an application."

"Hey Mick,," I interrupt. "You can hire him right now 'cause I quit."

And I smile huge.

***

The Amazon Room is packed tonight. It's karaoke night and all the models sing songs you don't want to hear in drunken foursomes. Drunk men wearing gold chains and Rolexes sing old country songs while everyone watches to see if they'll fall off the stage.

"Why don't you sing a song?" Chessy asks me.

"It's not my thing," I say and order another whiskey drink.

Then, this model with curves like a blow up doll struts up to the bar and orders a Jack and Diet Coke.

"Jack and Diet Coke?" I question.

"I'm on a diet," she shrugs and smiles down at me.

"You're so skinny, lady, I bet if I placed both my hands around your waist, I could touch both thumbs and fingertips."

"Fat chance of that happening," she says and walks off with her Jack and Diet Coke.

"Jack and Diet Coke?" I repeat in disgust, slugging the rest of my regular one down.

"I've heard stranger," Chessy says with authority and, almost on cue, an aspiring actor struts up to the bar and orders a *blow job*. Chessy laughs and I quickly learn a blow job is a Baileys drink served in a shot glass with a suggestive squirt of whip cream on top. I shake my head and leave her to flirt with the aspiring actor who slips her an Andrew Jackson.

The room's spinning and the only thought I can really fathom actually happening in actual reality real soon is vomiting. I pass by the fish tank near the men's room and stop to stare at a huge fish. It's a large, red one and it's looking straight at me with only one eye open. It swims gently against the glass looking like it wants to bite me.

Not far from the fish tank, near the entrance, is a big globe next to a fake jungle tree. The globe's almost as big as I am, and I get it into my drunken head that wherever my pointer finger lands is where I will move to. I spin it around and stop it with my pointer finger with my eyes closed. I open it and where does it land? Not the Caribbean, not Europe, not Asia, but Wyoming!

I walk back to the bar and tell Chessy I'm thinking of moving to Wyoming.

"What about your job?" she asks.

"I quit."

"I thought it was going well over there?"

"It's time to move on."

A minute of silence goes by, "My family lives in Wyoming. You can hang out with my brother when you go."

"Where?"

"Wyoming."

"What does your brother do?"

"He's a photographer. He takes family portraits."

"Cool. I might look into something like that."

Chessy writes down a number and hands it to me.

"What's this?"

"My brother's number. Maybe he'll give you a job."

"I couldn't do that!"

"Sure you could," she encourages. "Just call him."

***

Wyoming isn't that bad. I'm a photographer's assistant now. I take family portraits and Chessy's brother is really great.

We get all our business mainly by standing at the front door of a major grocery store chain offering discount photo coupons to Joe and Ma families from Wyoming who walk through the double doors.

The Joe and Ma families come through the photography studio and they'll say things like *These photos look so nice!* and thank you this and thank you that and I smile huge.

Chessy's brother is fat and watches football on the weekends. He invites all his friends and family over and we drink beer. When we go into work, he's constantly laughing and cracking crude jokes. He's heard all the ones from my *Skin and Flesh* magazines already.

When he shoots little babies, he plays with these

puppets and makes them laugh.

"I'm twenty-six and 'o on the babies," he tells me. Never once has he had a kid cry on him, or so he says. He's carved twenty-six notches on the wall to prove it. One day, we're going to make a documentary about his streak on my expensive professional digital camera.

He pays for my café mochas in the morning and even lunch sometimes. During happy hour he pays for all my whiskey drinks and at all the Go Go bars he pays for my admission. I'm not making the money I made in Hollywood, but my rent is cheaper. I live on a pullout couch in his basement.

Chessy came into town not too long ago to visit and somehow we started having sex in her brother's basement. Now we talk on the phone all the time and she asks me things like, "Do you miss The Amazon Room?" and I'll say, "No. I miss you, silly!"

The other night she said to me over the phone, "I'm thinking about going back to school."

"Where?" I asked.

"Wyoming," she said and I smiled huge.

AMID
MIDTOWN

EVAN HUNDHAUSEN

AMID MIDTOWN

It's mid-afternoon on a Friday inside an office building fifteen stories high. The building's lobby has a doorman. He's friendly and drinks coffee from a blue paper cup with a drawing of ancient Greek columns printed on the side.

I'm sitting on the top floor in the corporate headquarters of Juice Mungo in the "war room" where all the important things are talked about. There are only four of us here today. There should be more, but people have been getting fired lately.

Yesterday, I stood in front of thirty employees at the Juice Mungo production facility in Pennsylvania. They were all scuttled into a back office where I delivered the bad news.

"I will be happy to give you all recommendations on your job search," I told them. "You all have been given my business card. Just have them call me directly when you apply to a new job and I will give them the best recommendation."

I sat down in a chair and looked down at the carpet dramatically. The last thing I said to those thirty people was, "Honestly, I never want to be in this position again."

It was a lie though. This was actually the third time Tom the CEO has asked me to lay people off at Juice Mungo factories all over the metropolitan area in the last two months.

"It's the economy or something," Tom explained. "That's what they say in all the papers anyway."

This morning, over breakfast, I talked about the economy with my wife Elaine.

"The stock price is plummeting," I said. "Half of our savings just went in the tank!"

"It'll get better," she said.

"Those dark bags under your eyes make you look like a raccoon," I said as I lifted my coffee cup to my mouth.

"What a nice thing to say to your wife!"

"Raccoons are cute, darling," I reassured her.

I remember watching her place a plate with another pancake on it in front of Little Aaron, my five-year-old son. He ripped off a piece of the pancake and stuffed it in his mouth.

Back in the war room, on the fifteenth floor, I realize lobotomized people have more interesting things to say than the four of us at this meeting today. In boredom, I draw a cartoon skull with a snake coming out of its eye socket.

Irene, who's sitting next to me, notices my doodle and makes eyes at me. She's always doing this kind of stuff and it's annoying. It's even more annoying when I talk to her. Irene talks like she actually cares about her job, but it's easy to tell she's putting on an act. The only people who care about their jobs are guys who take pictures of Playboy bunnies and maybe some necrophiliacs who work in mortuaries.

The blouse she wears today is bulky and hides all the parts of her body that matter. It's hard to sit next to her because she smells like *White Rain*, which I like.

Butt Kiss Bill sits across from me. His hairline seems to be receding faster than the Indian Ocean before the tsunami. He puts his pointer finger on his lips as if that's helping him think. Overall, he reminds me of a dog who wants you to pet him.

Rumor has it he takes credit for things which aren't his. Irene is convinced. I could never take credit for naming a drink *Papayan Pleasures*, but I would gladly spend the outlandish bonus he got.

"We could add extra antioxidants to Berry Juice Mungo," says Irene to Tom the CEO. Tom sits at the head of the table playing with a rubber band not looking too concerned.

"Bottled Paradise has already done that, Irene," Butt Kiss Bill mentions. "We need to do something original at this point in the game, don't we?"

"Yeah, you're right, Bill," Irene says, sitting up and pushing her chair closer to the table.

I watch her blouse ruffle and gyrate as she scoots forward. Her breasts are *so* huge.

"If all we care about is the economics," I blurt out, "I think we should just raise our prices."

The three of them like this idea. I know because Irene and Butt Kiss Bill are nodding their heads like marionettes. The best way to keep my executive position I've noticed is to state the obvious. It's real easy to do.

I look at Tom the CEO as he sits there playing with his rubber band. I think of the Christmas party he had and his ninety-inch, 3D, back-lit, LCD, LED screen which sat above his monster fireplace. I think of how he watches the fine HD details of the green grass swaying on a televised golf game.

Tom and I played golf and drank way too much beer several weeks ago. We ended up at a topless bar and Tom gave a dancer one thousand dollars in cash for a private dance. When we left, he said, "I regret doing that."

I couldn't stop laughing at him.

Maybe Tom is as bored as I am in this meeting today.

"Hey, Tom,," I ask. "Have I ever told you I think golf is boring and I can't believe they televise it?"

Tom laughs heartily at my remark because he has a sense of humor. He snorts like a pig and it seems like snot might shoot out of his nose at any moment. Butt Boy Bill and Irene look at Tom, so they can figure out how to react to me.

Framed trading cards of golf players hang on the wall in Tom's office. I gave him an autographed one of a very famous golfer because I passed by a sports memorabilia shop called *Snarky's* on my walk home from work once. It was a way of thanking him for those golf games and parties I enjoyed going to so much.

I guess Tom and I are buddies in the most superficial way you can be when you work in an office. We watch *Ultimate Fail* compilations on YouTube. We order wings, cheese-steaks, and breakfast burritos together when we are hungry. During March Madness, we watched college basketball games on his office wall with the projector I set up connected to a laptop and some free TV website.

Several times we've made a game of trying to slip Ex-Lax into each other's coffee. We've both won this game before and there are no hard feelings. We just have more and more laughs making the time pass at work, even if the economy is in the tank.

Butt Humper Bill is jealous of our *bromance*.

"Take this meeting seriously, John," Butt Guster Bill says to me. "We have to meet with the investors at the end of the week."

"Why are you telling *me* this?" I ask, looking at Tom, who's stifling his laughter from my stupid joke about golf a minute ago.

Suddenly, the rubber band shoots off his pointer finger and it goes flying across the room. I have to laugh now too.

This morning, Tom told me about his twelve-year-old son Stewart scoring twenty points in his school basketball game. I told him about my five-year-old son, Little Aaron, trying fried chicken for the first time.

"The wife and I are real proud," I said. "You know how picky kids can be."

I left out how I turned him over my knee this morning and spanked him just because he ate his pancake too fast. He threw it up like the exorcist spewing slime. In hindsight, it would've made a great YouTube video. In hindsight, why did I spank my son for choking on his pancake?

"Where are you going?" Butt Plug Bill asks.

I have involuntarily stood up without thinking. Everyone looks at me like I'm going somewhere, so I say, "I have to go pick up Little Aaron from violin practice, but what I'd really like to do is go home, sit in my bathroom, and read that stack of *New York Times Weekend Editions* I've been saving."

I walk out of the office and head to the elevator. Once there, I wait for it to take me down to the lobby. I wave to the doorman and I exit the office building.

Today's weather is fantastic! It's like spring and I'm glad I walked out of the stupid meeting. I walk a couple blocks to the subway and jog down the steps like I'm going for the finish line in an Ironman Triathlon. Down the hallway to the train, I watch two female college students shake their hips to a dreadlocked acoustic singer playing Bob Marley songs.

"I read in the *New Yorker* some bum makes two hundred thousand dollars a year playing saxophone in the subways," I state, putting a dollar in his guitar case. "Do you get paid a lot playing tunes down here?"

"Do you get paid a lot with your suit and tie?" the dread man asks back, still strumming without a hitch.

I laugh and run to catch the train. Once inside, a weird muffled dingdong sound goes off warning that the doors are closing. It feels like I've just entered the Discovery One, the spaceship from *2001: A Space Odyssey*. I'm waiting for HAL 9000 to speak to me with its dry English accent. The subway car jerks along in rickety movements as it zips through the tunnel.

I start to think about all my problems as I sit there on the train.

How the hell is my son supposed to go to college when our stock price is going down? Then, people like Bozo Bill are coming up with stupid names like Papayan Pleasures?

I hold my head in my hands and wonder if I need to see a shrink. I've seen people break down before in other offices and they are never the same after. They get on prescription medication and nobody recognizes them. They've changed. Suddenly, they're like lemmings willing to go off the corporate cliff when just days ago they were just a little unpleasant.

I've visited too many Juice Mungo offices all over the country with people doing the same routines over and over, like worker ants feeding the queen, but dying of hunger. We all have juice shooting out of our rectums like a sixteen-inch gun on a battleship!

All the train passengers on board stare at the floor

contemplating private things. I take this moment in time to go over in my head how I got this far up the corporate ladder.

I started out in sales at Juice Mungo. I drove to grocery stores all over the metropolitan area in a minivan filled with poster board displays. I offered a fake smile and listened to store owners and grocery store managers complain about whatever they wanted until I finally got a chance to explain the pros and cons of displaying Juice Mungo paraphernalia in every inch of their store.

Sometimes, I even found out they weren't that different than me. Most times, I found out they had kids who needed things too. The biggest jerks would change their tune and pull out wallet-sized photos showing me little league pictures of their kids.

"Here's what you need to know about raising children . . ." they'd explain to me after we were chums. I'd then explain the pros and cons of hanging Juice Mungo displays around their store.

One time, an old lady who owned a small grocery market told me, "I collect mugs. I have many, many mugs. The trouble with mugs is that they break easily when you drop 'em, but I have mugs from everywhere; Disneyworld, Great Adventure, Water World, you name it!"

I found a box back at the corporate office, which was full of mugs with the Juice Mungo logo on it. I brought the whole box in just for her on my own time. The gesture made her day. *It really isn't hard being thoughtful!* I'd think, but wouldn't admit to when my co-workers asked me how I achieved such great numbers.

Sales wasn't much different than pursuing my wife

Elaine. I'd listen to her talk about whatever she wanted and then explain the pros and cons of us having sex. She once told me she liked Elvis. I found an Elvis action figure at a comic book store for twenty bucks. She kissed me for a full minute and then told me she meant Elvis Costello.

"You're a Looney Tune," I said and started chanting, "Insane Elaine, that's her name!" over and over while I tickled her.

Then I got her pregnant that same night.

Little Aaron was born nine months later and things really became nuts after that. I never experienced anything like it. In fact, the amount of time I spent not sleeping because I had a baby crying all night long almost made me jump off the Manhattan Bridge.

Every day I went to work. Once there, when I finished whatever it was they wanted me to do, I would ask for more things to do. I volunteered extra hours and I did tasks not in my job description even.

"Anything you need, just let me know, okay?" This was my M.O. after Little Aaron was born.

I told every higher-up I would be happy to do anything they needed. The company was growing a lot then and new positions were being created all the time, so I spent some time applying for them. It seemed every six months, I was getting promoted.

Often, I'd run into Tom the CEO around the office. I'd pass by and say, "Hi!" and he'd tell me, "I'm hearing good things about you, John!" Soon, I was training lots of people on how to promote expensive bottles of Juice Mungo juice.

A teenager on the train raps loudly across from me

while I'm thinking about my past. His cell phone blares hip hop through his headphones while he freestyles loudly along with it. None of the passengers nor I seem to mind.

I get off at the next stop and decide to walk the rest of the way home.

Outside on the street, I pass by a tattoo shop with a neon sign in the window that says *Tat Dat*. I go inside. There, I encounter a man behind the counter with small horns tattooed in India ink on the sides of his receding hairline.

"I got this artwork I want to show ya," I say. I hand him the doodle I made back at the office. He leans over and squints at it. "It's a skull with a snake coming out of its eye socket," I explain.

"I'll put it on your arm for one hundred and fifty bucks," he mumbles.

"Put it on my back for three hundred instead," I demand.

Recently, I saw a hot girl outside of the corporate offices walk by with a butterfly tattooed in the small of her back. I was standing there in front of the building with all the other guys on smoke break.

"Man, if only my wife would do stuff like that!" one of the guys said.

Someone else said, "Kinky."

Another guy began to say, "One time I dated this tattooed chick…"

I thought about quitting smoking just so I didn't have to listen to the guys talk about what they talked about on smoke breaks.

This is what I think about while the man with horns tattooed on the side of his head sticks a needle in my back. It's very painful, but somehow really exciting, too. When he finally finishes, I ask, "Where's the restroom? I have to take a number two."

"Down the hall," he says, lifting his eyebrows. "First door on the left."

I find it easily. I sit down to do my business and it feels like I have a really bad sunburn on my back. I contemplate what excuse I'll give my wife Elaine when she finally sees it.

It's my body, not yours! That's a good one.

I unravel the toilet paper roll. An autographed framed poster is on the wall in the bathroom. It's by some guy who figured out how to make tattoo images into a clothing line. I contemplate how I could rack up effortless dollars on eBay if I stole it.

I walk back to the front lobby of *Tat Dat* and pay the money I owe the tattooed man. I can't help but notice a girl across the room. She has a belt lassoed around her pants with fake metal spikes. The belt is bright blue.

"That belt she's wearing looks like a first prize ribbon for best booty!" I say to the tattooed man and he laughs knowingly.

I walk over to her. She has a hieroglyphic eyeball tattooed to her neck and her hair's dyed black as asphalt. Tattoo images are painted all over the walls with numbers. She studies them.

"So, these are examples of the images you can get tattooed on your body when you don't bring in your own doodle like I did?" I say out loud.

I see a frog image on the wall.

"Man, I should've gotten a frog tattoo!"

She looks at me. Her lips elongate and smile.

"Frogs," I elaborate. "They're cool. They go *ribbit*."

One of her eyebrows crooks in interest as if I've discovered a universal truth.

"It's not too late to get a frog tattoo," the tattooed man yells across the room at me from behind the counter.

"Why don't you cock block me some more, dude?" I blow my lid at the guy. "A badly drawn skull and snake are etched into my back and it hurts! I've been impulsive again like when I had sex without a condom with my wife!"

I walk out the door. The tattooed man behind the counter thinks I said something funny because I hear him laughing as the door closes behind me.

I pass by a bar on the sidewalk. In the window is a yellow poster with black lettering on it taped above a neon beer sign; *DJ Cola - House Music Tonight! $3.00 Long Islands All Night Long,* the poster states. I see another one taped up on a traffic light post at the corner and contemplate ripping it down, taking it back up to the meeting at corporate and telling Tom the CEO, Irene, and Butt Mugger Bill, "Hey! Why don't we add some DJ Cola to Juice Mungo?"

There's a great move.

It would probably be a huge hit with Irene. Maybe she'd make eyes at me and invite me back to her office. There she'd take off her blouse and pull me close to her chest, so I could really smell the *White Rain.*

I pass by a hotdog vendor.

"Where do you piss?" I ask him.

"What?" He asks.

"I want a hot dog," I say. "But not if you pissed in the water."

He immediately dishes one into a bun without missing a

step.

"No, wait!" I ask again. "Do you piss in the water?"

"I piss in the bathroom like everybody else!" He shakes his head in annoyance. "You want the hotdog or no?"

"I'll opt for the soft pretzel," I say.

I smother it in mustard and when I take a bite, my lips burn. It feels like I'm batting down flames as I walk away. I wipe my mouth with napkins scrunched together in my hand and think of how I should've bought a can of soda even though I could buy a twelve pack at Costco for the same price he's charging.

A can of soda from a hotdog stand is too expensive, but Juice Mungo charges ten dollars a bottle for juice and that's okay?

I realize I should've brought this up at the meeting. I could ask Terd Burglar Bill why our products cost so much when a two-liter soda only costs ninety-nine cents? I'd blame Juice Mungo for all the young kids in the ghettos with bad teeth. Their moms buying pop because it's cheaper than milk or Juice Mungo orange juice with calcium in it.

Butt Buster Bill would just say, "Soda's easier to make and therefore cheaper," but I can't imagine.

I took the family to the Juice Mungo factory tour last month. We went in a company chartered bus to Pennsylvania with other families. The machines just shoot papaya pee, carton after carton, bottle after bottle.

We lay hundreds off because the Juice Mungo machine doesn't need them. It just spits and spits its phlegm and it won't stop! Who cares what we add to our formula as long as we're charging ten dollars for sixty-four ounces worth.

I remember how my son threw up on the floor in the middle of the tour and my wife took him outside. I got to drink little cups of Juice Mungo juice at the end of it all.

On my walk, I pass by an overpriced version of a convenience store. It's a fancy organic market slash espresso place. I step inside and they are selling tiny bottles of Juice Mungo next to the croissants and biscotti in a cooler near the counter.

I walk up to the drink case in the back and notice a hot jogger girl with sweaty, shoulder-length hair standing there. She's wearing gray spandex, matching support bra and has a neon pink mp3 player strapped to her shoulder while she studies the selection of beverages. Her hand grabs a twenty ounce bottle of Papayan Pleasures with 1000% Vitamin C made by Juice Mungo,

Butt Monkey Bill's drink. He's part of the Juice Mungo legacy now!

"Is that stuff any good?" I ask the woman.

"Not bad," she smirks.

In my imagination, I feel like she knows I want to pour the Papayan Pleasures all over her body, all over her ivory, marshmallow skin. I watch her calves pump her towards the cash register like two juicy turkey legs you scarf down at Thanksgiving.

Standing in line at the register, I think back on the number of women I've been intimate with on one hand. I realize I'm not ashamed of this since I've always believed in true love or lust, take your pick, but the problem is I didn't die in my early twenties like some rock stars do.

Then there was the time I had sex without a condom and oddly enough, I didn't die like Romeo and Juliet or go hide in the forest like Tristan and Isolde or die in a car wreck like Juliette Binoche and Daniel Day-Lewis in that movie, and it seems there was no third choice when it came to one life and two death, so it turns out the answer to the extra credit question was Little Aaron.

I realize I've never been HIV tested, but considering I can count the number of women I've been with on one hand, do I really need—

"Six ninety-nine," says the cashier. I hand him a twenty for my twenty ounces of Papayan Pleasures.

"Outrageous!" I yell loud enough for everyone in the store to hear. "Who do they think they are? Do they just sit around in their penthouses thinking up ways to politely rape and pillage us patriotic, hardworking consumers?"

Everyone in line has turned their eyes to different geographical parts of the market to ignore me. The cashier hands me my change and he's already helping the next customer.

I leave the store like nothing's happened and continue my walk.

I pass by a school playground full of kids with their jackets unzipped. They flap their arms like birds and scream, climbing up and down a jungle gym with a slide. If I were the teacher, I would make sure each kid zipped up their jacket even though the shock jock on the radio station this morning said the temperature is still abnormal. Mid-sixties, possible highs of seventy.

An Italian couple next to me argues as we stand together at a *Don't Walk* sign. They argue in Italian with Gucci bags under their arms. The Gucci store has security guards that buzz you in. I realize I've never been in that store or any one like it, nor have I ever asked Insane Elaine if she wants to shop there.

"But there's no tax on clothes in New Jersey," I hear her telling me. "Little Aaron needs new jeans. He's a growing boy."

Last weekend, the three of us picked out Levi's and decorated Little Aaron in crowded suburban department stores. We crept towards the Holland Tunnel in traffic while it rained on the windshield of the car. Little Aaron was in the backseat complaining of car sickness until he finally fell asleep on the shopping bags filled with his new untaxed Levi's. Elaine sat next to me in the passenger seat and stayed awake so I wasn't the only one.

My back starts to bake under my shirt from the sun and I feel my tattoo hurting. I decide to change my course and I walk all the way back to the office.

It takes forty-five minutes to finally arrive at the Juice Mungo corporate offices.

The small meeting has turned into a big one. Every department is in the large banquet room. I notice someone I know from the local sales office walking towards the beer keg. We must be celebrating something if there's a beer keg.

"Hey!" I say to Troy.

I knew him when he first started. He had cornrows then. Now, his hair's shaved short with a line etched on the side to part his hair.

Today he's wearing a button-down silk shirt. The frame of the pair of glasses he wears matches his watch. They are both the color silver and accented with tiny diamonds. I'm sure they're fake on his glasses and probably not on his watch, but I don't ask him about it. The watch is loose on his wrist and the metal band clicks when he moves his arm.

"I got the promotion, John," Troy says, shaking my hand.

"I know," I reply. "Congratulations!"

"I heard a rumor I got the job because of you. Thanks for the recommendation," Troy says. "Seriously."

"Don't mention it," I say. "I'm happy things worked out."

It's always an interesting self-realization when your opinion actually counts and decides another person's future. I recall the meeting that decided whether he would get the promotion or not. I forget exactly what I said, but it was something like this:

"You know, I think I've called you an asshole to your face before haven't I, Tom? You didn't even fire me for it! So, who cares? This is a non-issue. What we need to think about is what Troy is capable of doing for Juice Mungo. Personally, I've made many mistakes on my journey here at the company and I managed to become a higher-up, but I'm here because people saw something in me and that's what counts. Yeah, there's this other guy vying for the same position, this Jason guy everyone seems to like, but he's only been around for six months. From what I know about Jason, he has some dings in my book. What about that time he pelted a foam baseball at someone during office hours? Granted, it was made of foam, but this guy used to be in the minor leagues. I don't think that's a nice thing to do on the job. I think Jason needs to leave his pitching arm at home if you ask me. Attitude is everything for this position and I know Troy has a good one. I've watched him train other sales people and he's just great. He's a natural leader and that's what we need. Troy's been here much longer than anyone else in the sales department and he knows the position inside and out. It's a no-brainer if you ask me. Troy's got my vote."

This is what I said at the meeting that got Troy the promotion, but I don't mention any of these details to him. Instead, I fill a plastic cup full of beer from the keg.

"What's this shindig all about, anyways?" I ask Troy.

"I have no clue," he says. "But you'll never catch me missing a keg party!"

I look at the stage and see neon green and orange triangles on the projector screen. It's a pie chart projected from a laptop. Butt Muncher Bill is trying to focus the picture by turning the projector lens back and forth.

Tom the CEO stands on stage and plays with his laser pointer like it's virtual golf club. He's taking swings while he waits for the projection to clear up.

I slowly ease into a chair in the front row trying not to disturb my raw back and Tom begins to speak.

"In the next three months, Juice Mungo will introduce several new flavors, Carrot Cardio Compulsion and Peach Potassium Punch. We're also working out a deal with a well-known chocolate company. We can't say who yet, but we're going to make a new smoothie called Choco Peanut Butter Pass Out. These are exciting times for Juice Mungo!"

Irene sits behind me. She leans over to talk into my ear.

"I thought you were picking up your son?"

She's so close to my face and I want to tell her to plant her lipstick red lips on mine, but instead I say, "Little Aaron? I left him at *Abdul's Suicide Bomber Baby Daycare*. They promised me he will achieve eternal life with Allah."

"Have another beer," she says and winks at me.

***

I ride the elevator down with all the guys from sales after the meeting. We're all buzzed from the beer and laugh out loud at the jokes we make as the elevator goes down.

"*Choco Peanut Butter Pass Out?*" Troy remarks sarcastically. "I'm about to pass out right now!"

Laughter fills the elevator.

We arrive at the lobby and I wave to the doorman as I exit the building. Once at the subway, I jog down the steps, pretending I'm Silvester Stallone in *Rocky*. I pass by the dreadlocked dude still playing his guitar.

"Have you gotten paid yet?" I chuck a twenty in his guitar case and he smiles at me as I turn and head to the train.

I sit down inside the subway car and it begins to chug along. My head juts from left to right to the natural industrial rhythm. I bend over and put my arms on my knees because it's impossible to sit comfortably with the tattoo burning in the small of my back.

Twenty minutes later I get off the train. I walk a couple blocks and finally reach home. I tease my hand along the fat, stone railing of the brownstone. The dirty texture brushes into my palm as I walk up the stairs. I insert the key into the lock, turn it, and enter my house.

Anime cartoons yell from the TV and Elaine is in the kitchen at the sink running her hands through tap water.

"What are you doing home so early?" Elaine asks.

I grab both of her hands before she can wipe them on her apron. There are several cuts on her fingers just from preparing dinner tonight for Little Aaron and I. I put her fingers against my lips gently.

"I'm losing it," I whisper.

I see Little Aaron sitting on the couch looking at us.

"Come here, Little Aaron," I order.

He slides down the couch and darts towards us. His head bumps against my back and I wince. Next, we're all laughing like this sitcom where everyone runs to meet Daddy at the door when he gets home from work. Little Aaron mumbles something and runs back to the couch as if he's missed something really important on his TV show.

Elaine turns back to the sink. I watch her apply pink soap from a push bottle to her hands.

"Is that the soap from the shop where everything smells real nice?" I ask.

"All things smell nice in a soap shop," Elaine replies.

She turns back towards me and places her arms around me. Her hands slip under my blazer and she pulls my white shirttail out of my pants. One hand tenderly slips under the gauze covering my tattoo. I feel the damp wet from the palm of her hand. Next, she places her other hand on it and more coolness transfers over.

"How did you know?" I ask her as my back burns.

A SHORT STORY

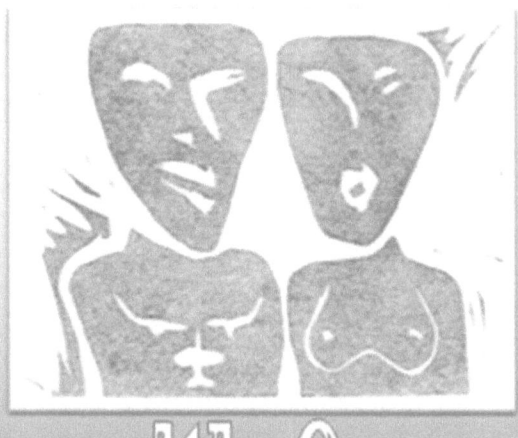

Keep with Company

EVAN HUNDHAUSEN

KEEP WITH COMPANY

She licks foam from her raspberry almond latte off a plastic fork. The foam is just like her. Light, but heavy at the same time. Heavy because she's my girlfriend.

Take the young man with a crew cut I see across the café for instance. He's leering at my girlfriend, Marina, as we sit together under a big red umbrella at a table outside the café. If I were him, it would appear to me that she's light, like the foam she's eating from a plastic fork, but I'm not him. I'm her boyfriend and for me she's totally real.

I remember Manny the Mac telling me over video chat that you take what comes with a relationship.

"You take it," he said. "There are no problems; just solutions."

Manny the Mac spent the last two months coaching me on women. Every week I spend one hour with him on Skype. He's a PUA or a "Pick Up Artist." There are videos of him you can watch on YouTube and he has lots of likes and thumbs up on Facebook and Twitter.

"Manny, I owe you," I said to him the last time we talked over video chat on Skype.

"No, you don't. You're paying me two hundred dollars an hour, remember?"

Manny the Mac wrote a book called *The Other Solution,* which I bought.

His book starts out like this:

There have been many books written about PUA all promising you sex with a different woman each night of the week. I don't know about you, but one girl is enough, isn't it? Do you need two dozen phone numbers? Probably not, but I'm getting ahead of myself. What's the other solution? Well, let me tell you. Many men I've coached have said they are too shy to talk to women, and are lonely. The solution for every man who has this kind of problem is partly talked about in this book, but maybe you feel I am describing you to a "T" and you want to get over the fear of rejection right now! Maybe you want to turn your life around and get a girlfriend fast! If this is you, then call me for a free consultation and I will give you the solution right away with coaching sessions over web cam. You won't regret it! Call this number today! (555) GET-GIRL.

When I called Manny and talked to him over Skype I was a little skeptical. He wore a silk shirt with several buttons unlatched at the top showing off his chest hair and a necklace with a peace sign during our first meeting.

"Tad, do this," Manny said. "Sign up for one coaching session a week. I guarantee you will get laid, get a girlfriend, or whatever it is you're looking for in no time flat."

Manny pressed the button on his vape pen and inhaled. He blew out a large vapor cloud at the screen and I could hardly see his face behind it. Then, I signed up for his coaching. I talked to him a lot about my problems in the beginning, so much so that we bumped it up to two sessions a week.

"Let me ask you something, Tad," Manny said in our earliest Skype session. "Do you have a job?"

"Yes," I replied. "I moved here for this job and I don't know anyone in this town and I'm really lonely."

"Okay, got it," Manny said. "How old are you?"

"Forty," I replied.

"Can you afford to take a girl out to dinner and a movie if you want to?"

"Yeah," I said.

"Do you live with your mother?" Manny asked next.

"No."

"Then you are in a better spot than ninety-nine percent of the men I coach. Okay, dude?"

A white kitten appeared on top of his computer desk. I watched it walk over his keyboard. He grabbed it with both hands and nuzzled it into his chest with a bear hug. Then Manny kissed it before he dropped it back onto the floor.

"Do you know what I do every morning?" Manny asked then answered his own question. "The first thing I do is look in the mirror and tell myself how awesome I am! Then, I think about all the girls I'm going to meet that day and how lucky they are to meet me. I want you to do the same thing every morning, Tad. Also, I want you to dye your hair."

"My hair?" I complained.

"I see a little gray there," Manny pointed at the computer screen. "You're forty. The big *four-oh*! Dye your hair. You'll feel more confident and girls will notice."

"Okay," I agreed.

"Then, I want you to walk down the street and say 'Hello, my name is Tad' to every woman you pass by on the street."

"What if they all think I'm crazy?" I asked.

"Why do you care what people think, Tad?" Manny said. "No one is thinking about you. Everyone is concerned about their own little life and the nuances of it. Not yours. Theirs. Say, 'Hello, my name is Tad,' smile, and you have won half the battle of asking a girl out just because you weren't scared like the other wimps out there. You're no wimp, Tad. I can tell."

Manny the Mac always knew what to tell me. Especially in the beginning, like when I failed to get a phone number from a girl.

"Do you know what Fortune 500 CEOs do?" Manny asked me once.

"What do they do?" I asked, listening.

"They never look at failure as a problem. They even word it differently. Instead of saying they failed, they say, 'I had a setback,' meaning they're on their way to finding a solution. You should look at what happened to you as a setback. Not a failure. Pat yourself on the back! You're talking to women and on your way to finding the girl of your dreams! You're finding solutions, Tad."

Yet, I still had problems despite his coaching. The more I tried, the more it seemed no girls wanted to talk to me.

"Pathos may not be your strong suit, Tad," Manny relayed one day. "Maybe it's more difficult for you than others, but who gives a hoot? Your motives seem pure and that's great stuff!

"I'll let you in on a secret," Manny confided. "Girls like sex as much as men do. The next time you're flirting with a woman talk about one of their body parts. Only one, not all of them. Just bring it up in conversation. You could say, 'Nice butt, now could you please pass the turnips?' You get the picture. If you comment on her beauty all the time, you will look like a pushover, but if you make an offhand comment about one of her sexier body parts, it'll get lodged in her brain that you want to do the nasty and not just be friends with her. It's a game changer. Give it a shot!"

Finally, I met a woman and asked her out following Manny's instructions. I made out with her one time and then she never answered my phone calls or returned my texts again. She went cold on me.

"This sucks!" I said to Manny on the verge of having a nervous breakdown that day. "She was so beautiful!"

"This type of behavior is called *ghosting*, Tad," Manny said. "Maybe she had buyer's remorse. Anyway, do yourself a favor and forget this girl. You don't want a restraining order on your hands. Trust me!"

Manny's white kitten appeared on the desk and poked its nose into the screen. He grabbed it off the desk with one hand and put it over his shoulder where it perched.

"Believe it or not I too have had my heart broken and I'm supposed to be the expert here!" Manny continued. "I've had all sorts of weird, unexplainable things happen, dude, but one day I finally realized how *awesome* I am and I've never got down about another girl again! Soon, you too are going to realize how awesome you are, Tad. It may take some time, but it won't take too much time because luckily . . . you know me!"

Manny was right. It took me a week to get over the girl.

I spent the whole time curled up in a ball in the fetal position. I didn't want to get out of bed and didn't want to talk to anyone, particularly Manny, but he wouldn't hear of it. He kept texting me, *What are you doing right now?... Call me!... How are you?... WTF?... Let's talk!* He wouldn't leave me alone and finally he gave me a free hour-long session because I was so depressed.

"I want you to do me a favor," he said to me during the free session. "First, shave your face because you look terrible. Then, dress up in a white button-down shirt, a pair of jeans and your nicest pair of loafers. Next, go out and get a haircut. Now, after you've done all this, go to the mall. Once you are there walk around and say hello to every hot woman you pass."

"I can't," I insisted.

"Yes, you can," Manny said back. "Get dressed up and go to the mall. Then, after you're done call me, okay?"

If I didn't have Manny the Mac to talk to during that time I may still be in my bed in the fetal position depressed. I owe him a lot.

Marina makes a statement interrupting all my thoughts about Manny and our video chat conversations.

"It's hot!" she says.

Her statement about the weather is true. I realize I've never told her about Manny the Mac and I don't feel like mentioning it to her now, either.

"Look at the skin under your arms," I say to Marina. "Look at how it jiggles back and forth!"

"What?" Marina lifts her arms up over her head to look.

This is called a neg and Manny told me to say these things to girls.

"I'm kidding," I say. "You're perfect in every way, except for the extra skin jiggling under your arms."

"Whatever, mister." She lowers her arms and goes back to her plastic fork and foam. The foam is almost gone.

During one of our sessions I explained to Manny, "I don't know how we started calling each other miss and mister, but that's what we're doing now."

"It's on, man!" Manny pumped his fist in the air. "It's called chemistry, Tad. Attraction, but whatever it's called it works! Keep it up."

I told Manny I had a problem with Marina's age during another session, but he put me straight.

"During Shakespeare's time, kings married fourteen and thirteen-year-olds, dude. What are you worried about? It's pre-programmed in her DNA to want an older man. Just like it's pre-programmed in ours to want a younger woman. It has to do with having babies, self-preservation, cavemen with clubs, and all that junk, know what I mean?"

"I think I do," I said.

"So, this conversation of dating a girl half your age is over, right now," Manny said. "It's fine to date someone younger. Totally fine."

"Well, let's switch it up then," I interjected. "Let's say I met someone who was forty and wanted to figure out how to date her. What would you tell me then?"

"I'd say old age is fine like wine," Manny winked. "Let me put it to you this way. Women are awesome. Period. Whether they are twenty-one, forty-one or eighty-one; they are all awesome, because they are all women! Okay, bonehead?"

I didn't like being called bonehead for two hundred dollars an hour, but I went with it anyway.

"We're going to change your name." Manny was silent as he thought about it. I could hear his white kitten meow in the background. "From now on, you're 'Tad the Bad.' It's your Viking name! You take what you want like a *Viking*!"

"Didn't Vikings rape and pillage?" I added.

"Hey, let's get something straight," Manny said. "I'm

not telling you to do that. I don't need a lawsuit, bud."

During another session I was still having problems with Marina's age. Our session went over an hour and I had to send him more money through the electronic pay site to stay on video chat with him longer.

"Tad, Tad, Tad . . . the Bad." It always got my attention when Manny said my name. "What you're thinking is nonsense. I've dated lots of twenty-one-year-olds. I've even dated eighteen-year-olds that had mothers my age. I've dated moms too, but that's another story."

"I don't want to date someone my age," I said. "I really don't. I don't like seeing blue veins on my own ankles and legs, so why do I want to see them on someone else's? Then, there are all those spots you get on your skin when you get older, freckles... It just goes on and on."

"You're right," Manny rolled his chair away from the screen's view. I could hear a snorting sound in the background. Then, he rolled his chair back into view, wiped his nostrils with his fingers and sniffled.

"Some women actually take really good care of themselves, Tad," he said.

"Really?"

"They go to Pilates or yoga classes all the time and have great looking bodies!"

"Where do I meet them?" I asked.

"I just said Pilates or yoga classes," Manny reiterated. "Are you deaf?"

"Well," I said to Manny. "I guess I should tell you. I met Marina's mom the other day. She's forty-five."

"Cool, you can date her if it doesn't work out with her daughter."

"Manny," I said in a serious tone. "This means she had

Marina when she was twenty-four. When I was twenty-four, I was applying to grad school, okay?"

"How'd her mom treat you?"

"She was nice to me."

"See?" Manny said. "There's no problem. Here you are doing the math in your head and no one gives a hootenanny! It's all good. G-o-o-d. The fact is you're more mature than Marina and she *likes* this, and you like the fact that she is hot and young. It works out for both of you, really. It's one of the greatest arrangements God has ever made! Older men dating younger women! Thank the Lord, Tad. Thank the Lord with me. Say it. *Thank you, Lord Jesus*!"

"Thank you . . . Lord Jesus," I said to appease Manny the Mac.

"There you go. Now, thank Ganesh and Shiva if you want to, but whatever you do, thank yourself. Pat yourself on the back and say 'I got the girl! I'm awesome!'"

Manny jumped out of his chair and began running around the room. He kicked his knees high in the air and pumped his fists. *Tad got the girl! Tad got the girl!* he chanted over and over. When he came back to the computer screen, he put his hands over his mouth and made a sound like a crowd cheering. Manny the Mac then stopped his act and smiled at me.

"Let's do this exercise," Manny suggested. "Inhale through your nose. Now I want you to let it out. Now pause your breath. Do you feel the impact this makes behind your eyes? That's oxygen going to your brain. Take another breath in and out and pause like that . . . There you go. Let's do it five more times . . . Now, when you're getting nervous because you're around the hot, young Marina or any hot girl for that matter do that."

I stop thinking about Manny and all our Skype sessions and watch Marina put a straw in her raspberry almond latte and sip. She looks up at me and smiles and I calmly look back at her. *Breathe in and out and pause.*

"You know, wars have been fought over smiles like the one you're giving me right now?" I say.

"Drink your coffee." She pushes her black hair back with her hand.

I notice one of her shaven armpits exposed by her sleeveless top. I think about what it would be like placing my lips on it. I imagine the texture of the soft stubble on my mouth.

"What do you want to do after this?" she asks. "It's such a beautiful day."

"Every day is beautiful with you in it," I say.

Marina grunts in disgust.

"I could say these things all day long and I probably will. Do you know why?" I ask Marina without waiting for an answer. "Because you're my baby. I don't know where you came from, but I am glad you exist."

"You know where I came from," she rebuts. "I met you at Walmart."

"I remember fondly," I say. "I was in the checkout line and you were a cashier. Then I asked you 'How's Walmart treating you?' and you said '*Horrible!*' making a joke. You smiled at me and I was impressed by your good attitude."

"You have a good memory," Marina says.

I realize that was a big night asking Marina out, so I decide to not say anything more and just sip my latte. I owe all the credit to Manny. He is the only reason Marina is with me.

I remember during a pivotal coaching session, Manny told me to ask Marina out to coffee.

"Do that," Manny said. "It's low pressure. Plus, remember to smile, Tad."

Out of all the things Manny ever told me, the hardest was when he said, "Don't tell *this* girl she's beautiful until she's in bed with you naked."

"That one's tough, Manny," I said. "I like to butter women up with compliments."

"Just take my advice," Manny conveyed. "You can compliment her all you want after you have sex with her, okay?"

You got to hand it to Manny. He really knows what he's talking about.

I take a minute to look at Marina's black hair and how the sun shines on it as we sit together outside the café.

"You know your hair is really brown?" I say, gently holding some of the long strands in my fingers. "I can see it in the sun. It's brown, not black."

"Really?" Marina asks, not paying attention.

She points to a video she's watching on her phone. "There are dolphin ladies crawling out of the ocean!"

"There's no such thing as *dolphin ladies*!" I say.

"It's a music video." She shows it to me. "It's one of my favorite bands."

My eyes light up when I see what's on her phone's screen.

"Those *are* dolphin ladies!" I say. Then, I change the subject. "Do you want a pastry?"

"A pastry?" she asks. "You mean a Danish?"

"I'll go get us one," and I get up and head to the

counter.

A song is playing over the speakers of the café. I remember the music video from the eighties. I watched it many times on MTV in my childhood. In the video, the lead singer chases some girl on a crowded beach in California. They have an argument and then break up in the sand. Then, at the end of the video, he sees another girl sitting on a towel smiling at him. They walk along the beach hand in hand. The video ends with a sand shark. Literally, a fin sticks out of the sand and chases some fat guy across the beach.

"Which kind do you want?" the barista at the counter asks me. "Cheese or raspberry?"

"Raspberry will be alright," I say. "It's my girlfriend's favorite flavor."

The barista is female, hot and young. Manny the Mac and I had a long discussion about barista girls at cafés once.

"Do yourself a favor and take the pressure off, Tad," Manny told me. "Talk about normal stuff like the weather. Look around and talk about something happening right in the moment. For example, if you are in a public place say, 'The air conditioner is chilly!' or 'It sure is cloudy outside!' or if there is music playing, say 'I love this song!' Are you getting the idea, Tad? It's called conversation. It's called small talk. Be yourself. I know you can do this. It's the easiest way to get to know women. You don't need any lines when you're being yourself."

The barista pushes a raspberry Danish on a white saucer across the counter towards me.

"I used to watch this music video on MTV in the eighties," I say, pointing up to ceiling where the music is coming from.

"In the eighties?" the barista says smiling. "Whoa!"

The barista takes my money and makes change in the register. She hands me my change and looks me in the eyes.

"I actually just bought this record at Barnes and Noble recently," she says. "The whole album is awesome!"

When I walk back outside towards our table the young man with the crew cut is sitting with Marina. It's always awkward when something like this happens, but it's okay. Manny has coached me on this too.

Once Manny said to me, "Gorgeous women are going to get hit on a lot! Even when you're dating them, it will happen. Don't be jealous. You should be flattered. Nothing is a problem when you are with a woman. There are no problems. Ever. There are only solutions. You're with her and she's with you. Problem solved. Capiche?"

I nodded. He never said *capiche* to me before.

"Remember," Manny told me. "Just like she gets hit on, because she is beautiful, you are a catch too and she is lucky to be with you."

Manny the Mac really knows what he's talking about, I think to myself as I sit down at the table under the red umbrella. The man with the crew cut nearly jumps out of his seat when he sees me.

"Tad, this is Eric," Marina makes introductions. "Eric, this is my boyfriend, Tad."

I extend my hand to shake his. Eric suddenly becomes formal and polite shaking mine.

"It's nice to meet you, sir." His grip is firm. He's

muscular.

"Eric is in the Army," Marina says. "And just got back from Afghanistan."

Marina has grown up in this town. It's a military town.

"Welcome home," I say.

"Thank you, sir," Eric replies.

"What are you up to now?"

"I've moving off base soon and I'm going to get a job. Maybe a sales job."

I pull out my business card and hand it to him, "Look up this company I work for. They have a sales team there."

"Thank you, sir." Eric takes the card from my hand.

I look at Marina and smile. Then I turn back to him.

"What did you do in the military?

"Army. Delta Force."

This is the first detail about this man that interests me.

"What was that like?" I ask.

"I can't talk about it, sir."

"I've heard that from other soldiers I've met," I state. "It just sounds so interesting."

"I'm only doing my duty," Eric says.

"I understand what you're saying, but I'm disappointed!" I laugh. "I like it when people tell me stories."

"I took an oath not to talk about it."

"I hear you," I say, nodding to him and taking a sip of my latte. "So, can I ask what you did in the army?"

"I was a sniper, sir."

What he says sparks my imagination. I visualize looking down the scope of a rifle in my mind. Another man is in the sight and gets shot. A line of blood spurts out the back of his head and he slumps over dead. Then, I imagine Eric putting the sniper rifle down and taking his Rambo style knife out. He carves another line in his helmet. Another kill. I want to ask him how many kills he's had, but he's already told me he's not going to talk about it, so I don't. Next, I imagine some general or colonel threatening to cut Eric's balls off if he ever talked about his *duties* in Delta Force.

"Why did you want to go into the army?" I ask Eric, figuring this question is innocent enough.

He surprises me when he says, "Video games."

"Really?" I ask.

"First person shoot'em up," Eric says. "I played *Global Military Tactics* a lot."

"I've played it," I nod.

"I was on a championship team," Eric reveals. "We'd go to other game stores and LAN gaming centers around the country. I went without dying for a whole session once. I just threw grenades at everyone. When I look at a map, I just know where all the opponents will be hiding. It's second nature. I turn the corner, put two bullets to the head. Done. The game actually prepares you to be a good sniper, too."

"Wow!" I say out loud, thinking about what he's just told me. "A *Global Military Tactics* national champion in the flesh! I was never good at that game, but it's cool you are."

"Almost everyone in the military is a gamer," Eric continues. "In the air force, the guys who play flight simulation games are the best pilots usually."

"That's crazy," I say, amazed by the information he's revealing.

I notice Marina is not paying attention to Eric or me.

She's paying attention to her phone and swiping the screen with her finger. There is a moment of uncomfortable silence. It is no big deal to me, though. I got the girl.

Manny the Mac told me during one of our sessions, "Remember, Tad, it's like a poker game. You can raise the stakes, bluff, even fold if you want to, but in the end, you win. You got the edge because you have the girl. These other jealous dudes don't. Let them hit on her. It won't get them anywhere."

Manny the Mac is a smart man.

"Well, it was nice talking to both of you," Eric the soldier says. "Have a great day."

He stands up and politely shakes Marina's hand. Then, he shakes mine and makes towards the exit of the café. I wonder if he could use Manny the Mac's coaching as I watch him walk away.

"He was interesting," I say to Marina.

"Yeah," she says, mesmerized by the screen on her phone.

She attempts to take a break from it and looks at me, but this does not last and she goes back to it. I'm tempted to ask Marina what she and Eric talked about while I was gone, but I don't. There are no problems. Another song from the eighties comes on over the speakers of the café. It's a rock ballad about love. Love was the subject I contemplated on many a sleepless night when I was trying to figure out how to ask Marina out.

"There's nothing to figure out," I remember Manny the Mac saying to me. "You're like a stewardess on an airplane. You ask the people on the plane, 'Would you like a drink?' and they can choose to say yes or no, but instead you're asking a girl out."

Manny makes things easy. I'm indebted to him.

He taught me how to text Marina with his *52 Pick Up Texts that Will Get You Sex Tonight!* download. You can go to his website MannytheMac.com and download it there. Marina didn't have sex with me the first night I texted, but she did the next night. Seeing and touching her body was the most exciting thing that had happened to me in years. Just her ass alone--

"Hahahaha!" Marina laughs at something on her phone. Probably a meme on Facebook. I don't ask her to show it to me.

"Every time I hear your voice, it's like music to my ears," I say to Marina.

"Shut up already!" she says, smiling playfully, but still concentrating on her phone.

I scoot my chair closer to her and move my fingers up and down her back. Gently I go up her spine and over her shoulder blades. I lean over and whisper in her ear something Manny taught me to say to get a woman aroused. It works, because Marina finally puts her phone away.

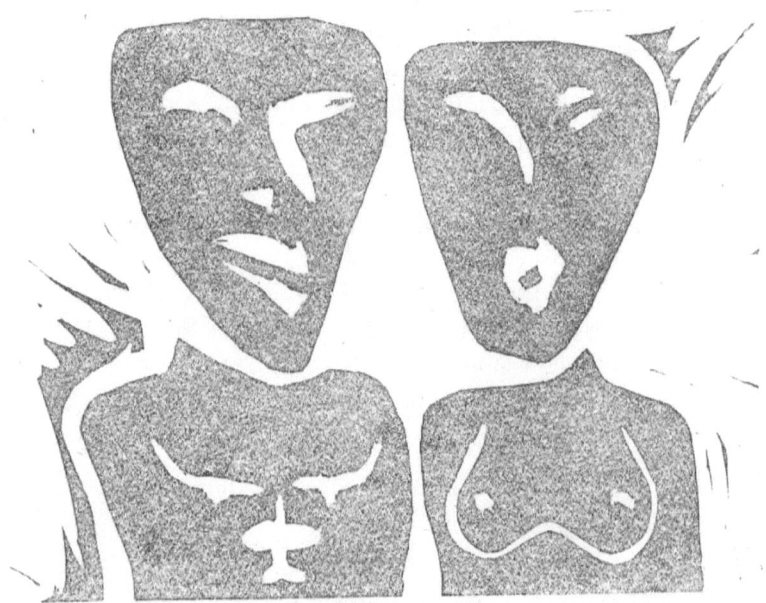

About the art: The above print by **Evan Hundhausen** was done on letterpress somewhere between 1999 and 2001, during a workshop at Naropa University in Boulder, Colorado.

Buy the postcard at:

http://www.zazzle.com/theboulderdj*

The
Other
Solution
by Manny the Mac

The Companion Book to a Short Story
by Evan Hundhausen

THE OTHER SOLUTION
BY MANNY THE MAC

The Companion Book to *Keep with Company*, a short story by Evan Hundhausen.

WARNING! This book is not dating advice. It's a work of fiction.

INTRODUCTION: So Who the F' am I?

Hi there. You bought this book thinking it was the answer to all your girl problems. But before I get started, let me introduce myself. My name is:

Manny the Mac; PUA coach, celebrity, and author of the international best-selling book *The Other Solution*.

What's so good about this book? you're thinking. Nothing really. Maybe you'd get better information from talking to a therapist twice a week. It's totally possible, but instead, let's just say for a moment you're actually serious about this topic and looking for solutions to your girl problems.

You may have noticed there are many books written on dating all promising you sex with a different woman each night of the week. Do you need two dozen phone numbers? Probably not, but I'm getting ahead of myself. What's the other solution? Well, let me tell you.

*Note from the publisher:

Since the publishing of Keep with Company *by Evan Hundhausen, Manny has become an overnight celebrity. He's not taking on any more clients. He spends his time living off the royalties of his book sales in exotic locales and is off the grid.*

Now that we got all that out of the way . . .

It's very possible since you're reading this book that you woke up today realizing there's something missing in your life. Then you went on your usual routine; the coffee run, the jog, then going to your job all the while thinking, *Good Lord! I wish I had a woman!*

Personally, this is what I've thought about non-stop since puberty. The amount of confusion I've had over this one subject alone has been a monumental burden. I screw up with women constantly, on a daily basis. Not all girls like me, but that doesn't stop me. My solution to this kind of *bummer* is to laugh it off. In order to do that, I have a constant stream of *The Three Stooges* and *Abbott and Costello* running on every iPad, device, TV, and laptop I have in the house. I laugh it off and you should too if you really want to meet lots of awesome girls you can take out on dates!

So, what I'm getting at is don't feel bad about not having a woman. Feel good about it! Walk around town laughing and smiling about it and see what happens.

How could I possibly do that? you ask.

Well . . .

Change Your 'Tude, Dude

This is the most important subject we can talk about . . . attitude!

This requires taking the focus from what's going on outside of you and looking at what's going on inside of you instead.

How do you feel right now? Do you feel good? A woman will like you more if you feel good. That's for certain. In fact, everyone will like you more if you feel good.

Maybe you're into being depressed all the time and wearing black lipstick and white face paint. If that works for you, great, but everyone else who's not like that should stick with me here.

It's quite possible athletes feel good more often than the rest of us.

Athletes always feel good don't they? You see them on TV in their uniforms. They have all that damn energy!

Exercise is the easiest way to feel good.

Go run around the block! How do you feel now?

Get on the ground and give me ten push-ups, soldier! How do you feel now?

Not everyone exercises like an athlete though.

Some of us sit in our chairs all day long working on our computers.

Some of us eat junk food because we like it.

They say the subtlest of changes will lead to better habits and better character.

Have you ever seen an advertisement that said give us two weeks and your life will change? Well, it's true. Two weeks is all you really need to see some differences, whether you want to lose some weight, learn a language, change your attitude, or talk to some girls.

Let's get back to the most prevalent thought that lots of men struggle with.

I'm lonely. What's the solution to this one, genius?
Well . . .

Start Here!

I'm going to give you some instructions and I want you to follow them.

1. First, shower.

2. Next, shave.

3. Now, comb your hair. No hair? You don't need to worry about this part of the grooming process then. Lucky, you!

4. Now, put on a pair of jeans. Jeans, I said. No shorts or khakis, dude. Jeans like you see in the cologne commercials and in the magazines.

5. Do you have a button-down shirt that's pressed and looks brand spankin' new because you're saving it for a funeral? Then, put it on.

6. Put on the black suit jacket, too, if you want. You're stylin' now!

7. Now, unbutton a couple of buttons at the top. Show off your manly chest, bro!

8. Put on your pair of loafers. Socks or no socks. No one's looking to see if you're wearing socks anyway, unless you're walking along the beach or by the pool (Nice places to meet girls. The women there are in bathing suits!).

9. Now, look in the mirror.

Don't you look cool now?
Guess how many women are going to check you out today.

Lots.

What else, Manny? There must be more to it than just getting dressed up? you're wondering.

Oh . . . Do you think you need to memorize a bunch of line*s*?

There are plenty of books written about that stuff already, so go out and buy those. It's usually not a big investment. Type "how to meet women" into Google and YouTube and see what comes up.

In other news, I'll tell you a quick story, a myth, an urban legend. .

Talk to the Girl or Else!

There once was a kid who lived in the city. He had friends who were thugs, local hoodlums.

He spent his time in the neighborhood bar down the street listening to all their stories. One day, they were all standing around bullshitting and an attractive woman dressed to the nines walked in and sat down at the end of the bar. She smiled at the young man. All of his tough, hoodlum friends noticed this and one of 'em said, "If you don't go over and talk to that broad, we're going to take you out back and beat you up."

Hmmmm . . . what do you think the kid did? Do you think he whined, *I don't know how? I haven't read enough books on this stuff! I'm not a PUA! I don't know what to say!*

Hell no.

I think he learned how to talk to women because it was more fun than getting beat up by thugs.

In fact, in the past, I was this kid in lots of ways, but in the end, the only person who beat me up for not talking to girls was *me*! So, I finally realized it was more fun to talk to girls than beat myself up for not doing it.

You are that kid, too.

Now, I know how overwhelming fear is. As a coach, I'm

Evan Hundhausen

going to tell you to just *be afraid* and say hello to the hot girl at the end of the bar anyway!

Be very afraid.

Take a couple of deep breaths.
Now, tell that whiney voice inside your head you aren't going to listen to it anymore! The cool thing is, the more women you talk to, the more you'll find they are friendly and your fear completely vanishes.

Trust me.

You will be so happy you talked to that attractive woman at the end of the bar.

I'm too scared to try this! I'm still afraid, Manny the Mac! you're thinking now.

It's okay to be afraid. Just don't beat yourself up for it, dude. It's not the end of the world if you chicken out and don't talk to her. There's plenty more where she came from, bro.

Breathe!

Breathing is the best way to relax, so try a couple of deep breaths.

How do you feel now?

I don't know how to breathe, Manny!

Go to a meditation place, a Buddhist temple, a yoga place, join the gym locally in your own town. Sign up for a class every day, once a week, whatever it takes . . . do it!

You need to start *feeling good*!

Keep Talking!

I realized one day that I didn't know how to text girls, so I went to the bar and I asked the first girl I met there, "What's the right way to text this girl I want to take out?"

She had pigtails and a headband on and looked at me funny with these mean girly eyes, and she definitely had a frown on her face, not a smile.

Then she told me, "Just do LOL and smiley faces! It's not rocket science, *playa*!"

And that's what I started to do.

Then, girls texted me back. One wrote, "Brah!" and I was like, "What?" and then they all started sending me frowny faces and pet faces and whatever faces you can make with their phones! And I was like, "Whoa!"

Now, you need to learn something very important if you want a girl. Learn how to talk to them.

Today, I told this waitress at a café that she looked French. I told her, "It's your hair . . . No, it's your sneakers that make you look French."

Her sneakers were neon colors and she looked like she popped out of that old instructional French TV show from way back in high school, you know the one.

She said, "I'm not French. I'm Italian." And then all of a

sudden, I thought to myself, *Italian? That's hot! Mama mia! Mia mama!!*

Then, she came over to pet the Chihuahua I had sitting in my lap.

Pets are chick magnets and the café was dog friendly so yeah, I had a dog in my lap, but despite that, the moral of the story here is I talked to a girl I thought was cute because I wanted to. I didn't say anything smart or funny. I didn't shove the dog in her face. I just talked to her about what I was thinking. I said, "Are you French?" and she talked to me for no good reason at all. She wasn't even my waitress! I just thought she was cute with her French style haircut and French sneakers and wanted her to know it!

I think anybody can do what I did today. Don't you?

Pick up your phone and call one of your closest friends and talk to them.

Tell them you are reading this crazy book right now. Start a conversation. Practice talking.

If you are feeling bad about your girl situation, the best thing you could do is call your closest friends and tell them how you're feeling because talking to someone about your problems works.

Talk to anyone. A shrink if you need to.

I'm not a shrink, man. Sorry.

I'm just a schmuck who a wrote a book. What do I know? Why are you looking to me for advice anyway? *WTF, dude!*

But enough about me.

Just talk to *someone* if you are feeling bad! This is way important! If you don't learn to talk, I really don't think you will meet many girls.

Try going to a coffee shop. Go in there and order a coffee. Now you're talking! You're talking to the barista at the register. Nice!

To Feel Good . . . Do Something!

Do something. It's the solution to feeling good instead of bad. Do something. *Do it, man!*

CONCLUSION!

For now, I'm done giving advice on girls. This book is over. The End. You know all you need to know.

Meditate. Join the gym. Stop being so hard on yourself.

Now smile and go say *hi* to some ladies.

You'll be surprised at what happens.

JOSE

AND HIS

GUITAR

EVAN HUNDHAUSEN

A SHORT STORY

JOSÉ AND HIS GUITAR

José replaced the strings of his weathered guitar. He tuned the knobs with WD-40, then placed the guitar carefully back into its case, which was made of flimsy cheap cardboard. The thin torn pieces of the black covering rippled off it like autumn leaves.

José returned to his dorm room after class every day and played his guitar for the rest of the afternoon. He would jot down lyrics for songs he made up. The rhythmic vibrations of the strings made time unimportant to him.

José practiced scales monotonously. He thought of Jimi Hendrix and how he read somewhere that he used to practice scales every morning when he woke up. Jimi thumbing blues scales in the morning, devoted to his guitar.

The acoustic sounds José made filled the air. He would occasionally look up and imagine Jimi leaning against the doorframe, pursing his lips as he listened to José, nodding in encouragement. Sometimes, he would see Jimi even mimicking him playing air guitar.

"You need to get a Stratocaster, man," he heard Jimi say.

"I can't afford one," José mumbled. "Besides, if I master the acoustic first, playing the electric will be easy."

One of Jimi's eyebrows lifted in agreement as he inhaled on his cigarette.

"Tone it down," José's roommate said, entering the room. He sat down at his computer. "I have to do my homework."

His roommate began playing video games. José

continued to pluck inaudibly. The calluses stung against the coiled strings as he worked his fingers.

José's dampened guitar playing and the sound of his roommate clicking the mouse made a song José listened to.

***

"I need to get out of here," José said one day to Jimi.

"You just got to be patient, man," Jimi replied. "School is cool."

"No, it isn't," José insisted. "I hate college."

Echoes could be heard coming from up and down the staircase of the men's dorm he lived in. José's roommate entered the dorm room. Several of his friends followed him in. They held beer in their hands.

They did not offer José one as they opened the beers and began drinking.

"Drinking is for dummies," José said to his roommate. "My father died in a car wreck because he was drunk driving."

"Shut up!" his roommate said to José.

His roommate and his friends huddled over their laptops, playing their video games and drinking beer. José strummed Jimi Hendrix songs, sitting there on his bed.

"Let's go to Taco Bell," his roommate announced to his drunk friends, and when they went, they didn't invite José to come along.

***

Sometimes after class, José would play his guitar under a tree.

"What do you do when your fingers start to hurt?" José asked Jimi.

"You have to play through it, man," Jimi said, fingering

his air guitar. "If you want to be any good, at least."

José nodded and fiercely played his scales, concentrating on the sound he made and not the pain in his fingers.

***

"You play that thing too much," José's roommate told him one night. "It's like the only thing you do."

"It's the only thing I like to do," José replied.

"You're weird." His roommate reached for another beer out of his mini fridge. "I mean, you don't even play in a band."

"I will," José replied.

"Yeah, right."

José did not listen to the discouragement of his roommate.

"You used to play in empty blues bars before you became a legend, didn't you?" José asked Jimi in his mind.

"That's right," Jimi said back. "Just keep practicing, man."

José laid his guitar on the floor of his dorm room. The strings vibrated as the body of the guitar rested against the tiles of the floor. José left it there and went to the bathroom.

One of his roommate's friends arrived. He was drunk and just getting back from a party. He staggered into the room, stepping on the guitar's neck and snapping it.

The guitar made a terrible sound as the strings burst out from the wooden body. José's roommate and his friend decided to make themselves scarce and ran from the dorm, laughing at what had just happened.

José returned to his room shocked by the sight of his broken guitar on the floor. Why had he been so irresponsible as to leave it there like that?

He bent down and put the broken guitar back into the case and closed it as tears filled his eyes. He missed home and his family.

José imagined Jimi's face. Jimi looked at José as if he knew what had happened, but Jimi couldn't think of anything to say.

José looked away from Jimi and sat on his bed concentrating on the pulsing sensations coming from his callused fingertips.

Yes, I Wear A Man Purse

EVAN HUNDHAUSEN

YES, I WEAR A
MAN PURSE

I've tried to ignore it, but I can't anymore. I've been wearing a man purse! I own a bag with a bunch of smiley faces on it, and on the front of the bag, it says Smile Train.

Inside the Smile Train bag is my tablet, a pair of headphones, and maybe some DVDs from the library I checked out, but not much else really. Then, I started using the bag as a purse. Everybody knows the joke from the movie The Hangover with Zach Galifianakis. Oh, I'd say to myself, did I just buy a chocolate bar I need to save for later? And I would think how convenient it was to have my Smile Train bag in that moment. Then, there was the time I spilled coffee on my T-shirt in public and went to the bathroom to take that shirt off and button up my button-up. . . that was convenient too. Tonight, there's snow outside and I sit in this coffeehouse, listening to renditions of the most popular Lorde song sung by two young bearded guys with glasses and winter caps, a duo called Stone Heart, with a thumpy drum, an electric guitar, and a microphone, and, of course, my feet are wet because I didn't wear my galoshes and instead, I'm in my Walmart brand sneakers, so I take my socks off and it's in this moment that I realize when I place my folded up elastic socks inside my Smile Train bag . . . I wear a man purse! Should I get rid of it? Why on earth would I do that? My positivity coach gave it to me! Do you understand? My positivity coach gave me a bag which says Smile Train on it! But what I really want to know is- are teenagers going to make fun of me when they see me walking down the street? These are the consequences I must face. Have you ever asked a girl if she would carry something for you? Every male has done this to a woman, because if it wasn't with your girlfriend, it was with your mother, grandmother, sister, or aunt. By the way, in any zombie apocalypse, the person who owns a purse carries the ammo and that's a very important position. A bag is very useful, you see. But If anyone ever asks, I'll just say it's for my tablet.

BLOG POSTS

For more blog post and short stories from Evan Hundhausen

visit:<u>www.goshdarnblog.com</u>

SHAM PAIN

A Short Screenplay

EVAN HUNDHAUSEN

SHAM PAIN

FADE IN.

EXT. DIRT ROAD IN MOUNTAINS - MORNING

The sound of a car swerving off the road. A girl named SHAM PAIN sits on the passenger side of a NISSAN XTERRA that's wrecked. Tail lights blinking. A cut on her forehead. GUY FOUR is in the driver's seat. There's blood all over his face and he looks dead. Behind them, a SEDAN pulls up. THE BOSS, a man dressed in a black suit, red handkerchief in pocket, rings on his fingers, steps out of the sedan and loads a handgun. His face can't be seen.

SHAM PAIN (V.O.)
The fact is, my job isn't as easy as it seems.

The Boss steps up to the passenger side window and puts the gun against Sham Pain's head.

INT. MOTEL ROOM - NIGHT

The sound of a DOOR SLAMMING. Sham Pain has closed the door behind her and is inside a hotel room.

          SHAM PAIN (V.O.)
All I was paid to do was deliver
champagne.

GUY ONE, wearing nothing but a towel,
smiles at Sham Pain. His clothes are
strewn behind him on the bed he sits
on.

          SHAM PAIN (V.O.)
I'd just pour the john one glass.
That was it.

Sham Pain hands Guy One a glass of
champagne. Man sips, chokes, vomits,
then dies.

          SHAM PAIN (V.O.)
Maybe john is the wrong word for
it. They were just dead guys. Not
like I could call myself a
prostitute. I never got to have
sex with any of them.

Sham Pain looks down at the dead man
and sighs.

          SHAM PAIN (V.O.)
A friend of mine had told me
about this high-class escort
service she'd gotten involved

with.

A picture of a business card reads:
HIGH CLASS ESCORT SERVICE Call 24 HRS A
DAY (555) 555-ESCT

                SHAM PAIN (V.O.)
It paid really well and it looked
like easy money, but I had other
motives. I was horny.

EXT. SUBURBAN HOME - DAY

We see MOM and DAD looking into the
camera wearing conservative clothing
and arms crossed.

                SHAM PAIN (V.O.)
I blame my parents.

INT. CHURCH - DAY

We see Mom and Dad and Sham Pain as a
LITTLE GIRL, age 7, walking down the
aisle on a Sunday Mass, bending on one
knee, making the sign of the cross,
before they sit down on the pew.

                SHAM PAIN (V.O.)
They brought me to church every
Sunday. They enlisted me in
Catholic Schools all through
adolescence.

INT. CATHOLIC SCHOOL - DAY

A NUN gives the camera a stern look and
smacks a ruler into her own hand.

SHAM PAIN (V.O.)
Not to mention there are:

EXT. SUBURBAN HOME - DAY

MOM and DAD look into the camera.

MOM
Diseases to think about,
pregnancy.

DAD
Your life could go down the tubes
from just one little mistake.

SHAM PAIN (V.O.)
At least that's the story my
parents gave me to scare me into
not doing it.

INT. CHURCH - DAY

We see the Little Girl looking up at
the crucifix behind the alter.

                    SHAM PAIN (V.O.)
I used to sit in church and stare at
the crucifix and imagine a
giant man was wearing it like a
chain around his neck.

We see the crucifix on the church wall
turn into a chain around a MAN'S neck.
The Man is 19. MAKING OUT sounds are
heard.

INT. DORM ROOM - NIGHT

                    SHAM PAIN (V.O.)
In college everything changed. I
wasn't meeting any guys I wanted
to have sex with. I mean I did,
but they weren't exactly very
mature.

We see empty beer bottles on the floor.

                    SHAM PAIN (V.O.)
I fooled around with one guy I
met. We were both drunk. We
didn't have intercourse.

She pulls out a condom and he refuses.

                    SHAM PAIN (V.O.)
He wasn't ready.

The Man leaves the dorm room.

                    SHAM PAIN (V.O.)
I was.

INT. ESCORT OFFICE - DAY

A LADY sits behind a desk looking into
the camera. She wears conservative
clothes.

                    SHAM PAIN (V.O.)
So, I took my friend's advice and
called them. The lady who hired
me said:

                    THE LADY
It's not part of your job to have sex.
That's a decision you two
make on your own. If he's cute or
the passion strikes you, well,
it's none of the company's
business; it's up to you.

                    SHAM PAIN (V.O.)
They didn't do lesbian shit, so
it seemed like just what I
needed.

INT. HOTEL ROOM - DAY

THE BOSS sits in an armchair, smoking
long thin cigarettes. He is dressed in
a black suit with a red handkerchief
in his coat pocket. We never see his
face.

                    SHAM PAIN (V.O.)
My first customer was another guy
who didn't want to do it. He
offered me a new job doing the
same thing except with a twist.

                    THE BOSS
I'll offer you ten times your
usual pay.

                    SHAM PAIN (V.O.)
Student loans were on the
horizon. So, I said what the
hell. He gave me a free cell
phone with unlimited minutes. All
he wanted me to do was deliver a
bottle of champagne.

                    SHAM PAIN (V.O.)
I said:

                    SHAM PAIN
Don't you want a copy of my
driver's license? My social
security number?

                    SHAM PAIN (V.O.)
He said:

                    THE BOSS
No thanks. I don't even want to
know your name. From now on, I'm
the boss and I'll call you by

your codename, Sham Pain.

INT. DORM ROOM - DAY

Stacks of large bills are seen strewn all over her dorm room.

             SHAM PAIN (V.O.)
I knew right away I was getting into some shady stuff, but if you saw the cash I was getting. I had shitloads everywhere, under my mattress, piggy banks, in my sock drawer, coffee cans, cereal boxes, shoe boxes.

INT. HOTEL ROOM - DAY

             SHAM PAIN (V.O.)
Finally, I told him I needed a bank account. He gave me a phone number in Costa Rica. I received a debit card in the mail along with a letter every month telling me how much interest my account was earning. But I still wasn't having sex.

INT. MOTEL ROOM - DAY

GUY TWO wears nothing but a towel, pacing around the room, smoking a cigarette. Sham Pain sits calmly in a chair, holding a bottle of champagne.

                    GUY TWO
I need a drink beforehand. You
should loosen up and have one
yourself, but if you don't open
that bottle soon, I'm going to
the damn liquor store.

                SHAM PAIN (V.O.)
It was no use. It was like they
were all waiting for my delivery.

Guy Two pops open the bottle of
champagne, drinks, and dies. Sham Pain
touches the guy's bare chest. Then
backs off and walks out of the motel
room, bottle in hand.

INT. NISSAN XTERRA DRIVING DOWN THE
STREET - PASSENGER SIDE - DAY.

                SHAM PAIN (V.O.)
After a job, I had to call the
boss right away and tell him my
mission was complete. Sometimes,
he'd have more than one delivery
a night and I'd drive around the
county to motel after motel. It
was easy work, sometimes.

INT. MOTEL ROOM - DAY

GUY THREE sits in a chair wearing a towel.

> GUY THREE
> I don't drink, but you feel free to go ahead.

> SHAM PAIN (V.O.)
> The Boss always had a plan B.

Sham Pain pulls a bottle of sparkling apple cider out of her purse. Guy Three drinks and falls over, dead.

INT. COLLEGE CLASSROOM - DAY

> SHAM PAIN (V.O.)
> I managed to keep good grades only because the walls of the classrooms were cement and blocked all the cell phone signals out.

EXT. COLLEGE CAMPUS - DAY

> SHAM PAIN (V.O.)
> But once I left class, I was back to work.

INT. MOTEL ROOM - NIGHT

GUY FOUR wears designer winter ski clothes. Watches the motel TV.

                    GUY FOUR
You may not believe this, but I'm
immune to all sexual diseases. I
know it sounds crazy. I've had
over a dozen lab studies done on
me and no one can figure out why.
I'm just a genetic miracle. A
cosmic mistake on God's frying
pan.

                  SHAM PAIN (V.O.)
He was cute enough. But, like
everyone else, he couldn't wait
for me to open the champagne.

He pops open the champagne and gulps it
down.

                    GUY FOUR
Ahhhhhhh, that's good stuff.

Sham Pain waits for him to choke and
die. He doesn't.

                    GUY FOUR
Have some.

                  SHAM PAIN
I'm not thirsty.

Guy Four lays down on his bed.

                SHAM PAIN (V.O.)
For the first time, I actually
got my wish. Someone who was
immune to my poison.

They make love.

                SHAM PAIN (V.O.)
I was so excited, I forgot to
call the boss.

INT. MOTEL ROOM - NEXT MORNING

An alarm clock says 8:48 AM. We hear
Guy Four taking a SHOWER in the
bathroom. Sham Pain picks up her cell
phone and dials.

                OPERATOR
We're sorry, but the number you
are trying to reach has been
disconnected. If you believe you
have reached this message in
error, please hang up, and dial
the number again.

Guy Four walks out of the shower.

                GUY FOUR
Who are you calling?

                SHAM PAIN
My boss.

                    GUY FOUR
Don't worry about that. I already
did.

                    SHAM PAIN
What?

                    GUY FOUR
Yeah, I rented you out for
another couple of days. Your boss
said it was all right. I'll make
it worth your while, I promise.

INT. HOTEL ROOM - DAY

The Boss hangs up the phone and
violently extinguishes his slim
cigarette. He gets out of the chair and
leaves, turning the light off.

                SHAM PAIN (V.O.)
When you disobey your mom or dad
and stay out too late, and know
you will get in trouble the next
day, at times like that, there's
no need to feel guilty, you just
have to go forward with it and
have fun. No matter what you do,
you won't be able to avoid the
consequences, which eventually
have to come.

INT. MOTEL RESTAURANT - MORNING

A WAITER pours a bottle of champagne
into two glasses of orange juice. Puts
them on a tray and brings them out to
Guy Four and Sham Pain.

          SHAM PAIN (V.O.)
My new boyfriend wanted me to
stick around so he could have a
skiing partner up in the
mountains. I was flattered. I
even thought the boss might
forget all about me.

EXT. DIRT ROAD IN MOUNTAINS - MORNING

A Nissan Xterra drives along a deserted
dirt road in the mountains. Sham Pain
and Guy Four are smiling and laughing
in the car. He grabs her hand and puts
his fingers around hers. The Boss
stands on a hillside with a sniper
rifle and FIRES a bullet at the Nissan.

          SHAM PAIN (V.O.)
We were on our way to the ski
resort when a tire was shot out.

The Nissan Xterra swerves off the road.
CRASHES into a tree.

INT. NISSAN WRECKED ON THE SIDE OF THE

ROAD - DAY

Sham Pain sits on the passenger side of
the wrecked Nissan. Tail lights
blinking. A cut on her forehead. GUY
FOUR is in the driver's seat. He is
bleeding from his head and looks dead.
Behind them, a sedan pulls up. The
Boss, a man dressed in a black suit,
red handkerchief in pocket, rings on
his fingers, steps out of the sedan and
loads a handgun. His face can't be
seen.

                SHAM PAIN (V.O.)
I'd seen so many men dead on the
floor because of me. They died
alone, squirming and choking on
the floor, looking at me in
disbelief as I watched. I don't
know what happened to my Costa
Rican bank account. I don't know
what happened to the cell phone.

The Boss reaches into Sham Pain's purse
and pulls the cell phone out and
pockets it.

                SHAM PAIN (V.O.)
I don't even know what happened
to that business card my friend
gave me.

The Boss puts the handgun to her head.

                    SHAM PAIN (V.O.)
I'm not going to sit around and
rationalize it. It was just one
of the many little cosmic
mistakes in God's frying pan.

She opens her eyes. She looks faint. We
see her holding hands with GUY FOUR.
There is blood on their hands. The Boss
decides not to shoot her in the head.
He gets back in his sedan and drives
off.

                    SHAM PAIN (V.O.)
Then all of a sudden.

GUY FOUR catches his breath and coughs.
He's not dead.

                                        FADE OUT.

                    THE END

ABOUT THE AUTHOR

Evan Hundhausen graduated from Naropa University in 2001 with an MFA in creative writing.

He has written for magazines like THC: The Hemp Connoisseur, Dope Magazine, DMC World, and Colorado Music Buzz.

Visit www.goshdarnblog.com and www.djcola.net to learn more about him.

Help by Reviewing This Book on Amazon!

YOUR FREE GIFT

As a way of saying **thanks** for your purchase, I'm offering a free e-book for readers.

I've learned a lot about writing fiction over the years. If you're interested in learning as well, then I recommend checking out

10 Ridiculously Simple Ways to Write Fiction Better!!

http://eepurl.com/bMiszH

Download and enjoy today!

FASHION STORE

Do you like T-shirts? Watches? Hats? Wallets? Postcards?
Buttons? Hoodies? Hand Bags? Phone Cases? And more?

Then head over to the shop on Zazzle and check out these
fashionable designs.
zazzle.com/theboulderdj

www.ingramcontent.com/pod-product-compliance
Lightning Source LLC
Chambersburg PA
CBHW031112260626
47172CB00001B/335